LOADED COLT

Lawman Lee Masters was surprised when he learned that his brother had left him his ranch – surprised that there was any ranch to leave – but bigger shocks were in store for him. He discovered the ranch was poverty-stricken, and his brother had been a rustler who had been murdered by the gang. What Lee had inherited was trouble, but this was one thing he always faced and soon the range was ablaze with gunsmoke. Lee's guns left leather many times before the evil that oppressed the range at Lansing was wiped out for ever.

LOADED COLT

LOADED COLT

by

Mark Donovan

Dales Large Print Books
Long Preston, North Yorkshire,
BD23 4ND, England.

British Library Cataloguing in Publication Data.

Donovan, Mark
    Loaded Colt.

    A catalogue record of this book is
    available from the British Library

    ISBN   1-84262-410-5 pbk

First published in Great Britain in 1960 by Robert Hale Limited

Cover illustration © Faba by arrangement with
Norma Editorial S.A.

The moral right of the author has been asserted

Published in Large Print 2005 by arrangement with
Robert Hale Limited

Dales Large Print is an imprint of Library Magna Books Ltd.

Printed and bound in Great Britain by
T.J. (International) Ltd., Cornwall, PL28 8RW

Chapter 1

Lee Masters put his deputy's badge gently down on Sheriff Bentley's desk. 'Sorry Dan,' he said, 'but you knew I'd be leaving you sometime, and my brother willing me his ranch has just made it sooner, that's all.'

Sheriff Bentley sat right back in his chair, his feet on his desk, his shrewd grey eyes quizzing his ex-deputy.

'Coincidence Purdy should have a ranch up at Lansing, ain't it?'

Lee shrugged his broad shoulders, shoulders which tapered to the narrow waist and hips of a man who had spent most of his time in the saddle; a twist to his good-humoured mouth suggested that he did not find the coincidence a particularly pleasant one. 'A queer set-up all round,' he said.

'Hadn't heard from your brother in years had you, Lee?'

'Naw, we never did get along; he bossed me when we was kids and I never took to being bossed.'

'So I figured,' Dan replied cuttingly. 'If you'd done what I told you just twice out of ten times I guess you might've turned out something like a deputy. Well, I'm rid of you now you've got yerself a ranch.'

'You ever run across this attorney that wrote me from Lansing?'

'No, can't say I have, Lee. Fact is, all I knows about Lansing is that it's a tough place with not much law – that's what surprised me when I heard he'd put up his shingle there.'

'No more surprising than me inheriting like I have. I'd heard he was married,' Lee said.

'He was, huh? Maybe they didn't get along – no more than you an' Laurel would've.'

'Dan, you keep your tongue…'

'Easy, feller,' cut in Bentley. 'Old man like me's got a right to say what he thinks, and that is that you should be real glad Purdy come down here to buy heifers and took her an' all.'

An angry scowl marred Lee's usually pleasant face, his grey eyes were as cold as ice– 'I ain't taking that from no one, Dan.'

'Hold on, son, maybe I spoke out of turn, but it had to be said. Sure, Laurel's a right handsome gal, but…'

'Save it, Dan. I'm buying a drink. You coming?'

'Be along soon Lee. Just one or two things to do first.'

Lee nodded, moved out of the adobe office into the crushing heat of the street and along to the 'Signal' where half a dozen noon-time drinkers greeted him cheerfully and asked him to 'likker'.

'My treat, boys. I'm leavin' town!'

'Quittin', Dan?' the bottle-nosed saloon keeper queried.

'Just that, Al. You kin throw your own drunks and tinhorns out from now on; I'm headin' North.'

'Wouldn't be headin' for Lansing would you, Masters?'

Lee turned with deliberate slowness to face his questioner who had just pushed through the swing doors into the 'Signal'. – 'What's that to you Purdy?' he demanded with dangerous quietness.

''Cause I don't want no second-hand Deputy Sheriffs hangin' around my part of the country! And I don't want you sniffin' round Laurel no more!'

To Lee it seemed that now, for the first time, he was seeing Purdy as he really was, and not liking what he saw any more than he had liked it before. Duke Purdy was a big fellow, well set up with a floridly handsome face, a thick neck and broad shoulders; he had come south to Tracy to buy pedigree cows from old Meredith whose breed were famous in that part of the South-west. While in Tracy he had lost no opportunity of impressing upon its inhabitants just how important, popular and wealthy Duke Purdy was; among the few who had taken him at his own value was Laurel Anderson, daughter of the store-keeper and acknowledged belle of Tracy. Lee Masters had been courting her with indifferent success and many rivals for some months, and had not been pleased with Purdy's almost immediate success– 'I'll ride where I want, Purdy,' Lee stated curtly, 'and I'll not be needin' permission from no big mouthed jay, neither!'

Purdy's face flushed– 'Where I come from…'

'Them are shootin' words,' Lee cut in. 'Sure I know. What of it?'

He realised abruptly that he had gone further than he intended; he knew that Purdy was reputed to be fast with a gun, but since he also knew that that reputation was largely self-advertised it didn't worry him at all; he had full confidence in his own skill with his own two well used Colts. But, after all, Laurel loved the coyote, and he wasn't wanting to spoil her marriage before it had begun. Purdy must have sensed Lee's hesitation for a sneer quirked his full mouth, his hands poised over the pearl-inlaid butts of the two Colts he wore–

'Wanna make somethin' of it, Masters?' he demanded. 'Folks aroun' here seem to figure you're a fast man with gun. Are you?'

Lee stared into Purdy's eyes– 'Don't crowd me, Purdy,' he advised quietly.

10

'Hey! Hark at him!' Purdy sneered, 'Makes a big noise with his mouth but when it comes to the point he backs down. Awright, loud-mouth, just remember what I said. Don't go sniffin' round...'

And then Lee hit him; he moved as quickly as a mountain lion and his bunched right hand smashed into Purdy's mouth; Purdy went lurching back, the heel of one of his hand-tooled leather boots caught in a knot-hole and he thumped on the floor. Instantly he gathered himself, his right hand darting to a gun, but Lee moved as quickly, kicked the one Colt out of his hand, snatched the other from its holster and tossed it away into one corner of the saloon. Then he stood back, unbuckled his own gunbelts and handed them across the bar only a second before Purdy catapulted from the floor and rushed at him with flailing arms. Lee took one punch on the ear that made his head sing, another under the heart that made him gasp, then he bored in, both hands busy snapping short, hard punches to Purdy's ribs and stomach. Purdy was tough; he fought back hard and Lee took a lot of punishment before he was able to pick one off the floor and land it flush on Purdy's chin. Purdy's head jerked back, he grunted, and his guard dropped. Instantly, Lee put his full weight into a left hook to Purdy's stomach before bringing over a haymaker right which dropped the big man like cold meat.

Lee staggered to the bar, his face a mass of blood from a cut eyebrow, his lungs gasping for breath– 'How's about that drink?' he managed to grunt. He had just got the drink to his bruised lips which smarted at the sting of the whisky when the glass was knocked out of his hand and his head rocked to one side under the impact of a full arm slap; he lurched to one side–

'Bully!' Laurel shouted at him. 'Coward! Pickin' on Duke thataway!'

Lee raised a protesting hand, even at that moment thinking that Laurel looked even more lovely when she was angry; evidently someone had hurried across to her father's store to tell her Duke and Lee were scrapping, for she still had flour on her hands and arms, some of which had been transferred to Lee's face– 'Hey, Laurel!' Lee protested. 'It was him picked on me!'

'A likely story! Don't you ever dare to speak to me again, Lee Masters! I hate you!' She stamped her foot, then as Purdy regained consciousness with a groan, she ran to him and helped him up, wiped the dust from his expensive clothes and gave him her shoulder to lean on as, after a venomous glance at Lee, he dragged himself out of the 'Signal'.

Dan Bentley swung his bulk up to the bar, reached under it for the special bottle that was kept for him and poured himself a drink–

'My guess, Lee,' he advised, 'is you better be careful up in the Lansing country. Here's luck. You'll be needin' it!'

Chapter 2

At first sight, Lansing looked pretty much like any other cow town, but to Lee Masters it looked pretty good. He had been four days on the trail, four days of hard riding over rough country, under a blazing Arizona sun which did its evil best to suck every drop of moisture out of his body and to fry his brain. He knew he'd made good time, and had meant to do just that for, for some reason he couldn't have adequately explained, he wanted to get to Lansing before Purdy. All the way, while he was pushing his big, long-striding black as fast as he dared, there had been a doubt nagging at the back of his brain, a doubt about the errand on which he had set out. Lee Masters' youth had been a hard one; brought up on a Texas scrub ranch that had barely paid its way and his father's drink bills, he had had to work nearly as soon as he could sit a horse – and that wasn't so long after he had learned to walk. Work had left little time for schooling; he could read – just, and write his name with difficulty. Like many nearly illiterate people he was suspicious of the written word and the letter from the law-sharp in Lansing who

14

signed himself – 'Edward Cowin, Attorney-at-Law,' hadn't somehow inspired him with any confidence; perhaps it was because the letter had contained so many words the meaning of which Lee could only dimly understand. He'd read it so often, he knew it off by heart; cutting out Cowin's long-winded verbiage, it told Lee that his brother was dead and had left his Circle M ranch to him. Beyond that, in spite of the number of words, there was no information at all; Lee had no idea how, or even where, his brother had died, nor had he any idea of what sort of ranch he had inherited.

Lansing, drowsing in the blistering heat of the early afternoon sun, looked shabby; little paint had been used in recent years on the cracked and sun-warped wood of the store fronts or saloons; only one building looked substantial, it was brick-built and boasted the only genuine second storey and bore a faded, sagging notice– 'Court-house and County Jail'. In the shade, off to one side, a few fowls searched dispiritedly for food among the litter of cans which bestrewed the alley. Outside the 'Red Dog' a cow pony stood, head drooping in the heat, tail flicking at the flies which bothered him; in one window of 'Dobie's Cattleman's Hotel and Eatery', a curtain moved a fraction and a beady eye peeped out. These movements apart, Lansing could have been a dead town;

in Hughes' livery stable, Lee found a man asleep in an old rocker, a fat man who slept uneasily, bubbling snores disturbing the flies which explored his face; he didn't wake up when Lee led his black to a stall, unsaddled and rubbed him down before forking a feed of hay into his manger. Shouldering his saddle, Lee tramped back to where the fat man slumbered under the entrance arch, prodded the sleeper with an ungentle toe. The fat man woke with a start, grabbed clumsily at a gun which hung from his waist–'Easy, feller,' Lee warned him, 'ain't no call to git vi'lant!'

The fat man cleared his throat raspily, his eyes were bloodshot and his lips trembled–'Who'n hell are you?' he demanded, in a voice so thickened by whisky as to be barely understandable.

'I just hit town,' Lee told him. 'Put me horse in a stall.'

'Buck a day it'll cost you – in advance.'

Lee fumbled out a five-spot– 'Be long enough,' he said, and poked the folded note into one pocket of Hughes, sagging, unbuttoned vest.

'Stranger, huh?' Hughes queried, his tone slightly less unfriendly by the sight of the sawbuck.

'Yeh. Hotel in town?'

'Dobies. Only place. Clean, but no likker, his old woman's agin it. You a drinkin' man?'

'Take one now and then. You?'

'Feller, the drink I've had would reach from here to China. Y'know, I had me a big ranch once? Fact! Ran near twenty thousand head. I sure did, and was so pleased with myself I took a drink to celebrate, first drink I ever took! But not the last. Soon I was down to ten thousand head – and then...' His lachrymose voice still rumbled on as Lee eased himself out into the street and along the board-walk to Dobies. Once again the curtain twitched, and inside the entrance hall he found himself face to face with the owner of the beady eye, a small, grey-faced, dried-up woman with a thin gash of a mouth; hands folded, she looked at him with the deepest suspicion–

'Yeah?' she queried, the voice was acid as an unripe gooseberry.

'I need a room, ma'am,' Lee told her, sliding his hat off his head.

'Stranger?'

'Yeh. Just hit town.'

'Two bucks a day – in advance.'

'Seems like you don't trust nobody in this town!' Lee smiled. 'I just had to pay livery in advance too.'

Mrs Dobie's dark eyes sparked angrily– 'That Hughes! Drunken no 'count loafer! Drinks!'

'Yeah, so I guessed. Had a big ranch once – he said.'

17

'Liar! Never owned a chicken coop! He don't even own the livery; just works for Earl – loafs rather. Two bucks a day, in advance, young feller, and I'll have no drunks in this house!' She spoke with such determined aggression that Lee very nearly chuckled, but managed to get his face under control and told her–

'I ain't no drinkin' man, ma'am. And here's two bucks.'

'Stayin' in town?' she asked as she almost snatched the two bills which instantly vanished into one of her many pockets.

'I got business here, ma'am, which will maybe take me a couple o' days to sort out.'

'What sort o' business?'

'Right now, ma'am, my most urgent business is to get washed up. I come quite a ways today and I'm plumb dusty.' He spoke quietly but his firm tone brought a faint flush to her pallid face and made her thin lips tighten–

'Room's thisaway,' she snapped.

The room was small and sparsely furnished but spotlessly clean, a clean towel hung by the hand basin, the jug contained clean water and there was a new cake of soap in the dish– 'Sure looks good, ma'am,' Lee praised as he dumped his saddle in one corner of the room.

'It's clean now, young man. See you keep it that way,' Mrs Dobie snapped ungraciously, and marched out.

Lee washed the dust from his face, had a quick shave and then remembered he was hungry; back in the hall, he knocked on the door leading to the room from which Mrs Dobie had watched him, then entered in response to her– 'Come in.'

He found himself in a room so crammed and cluttered with furniture it was fully a minute before he could see Mrs Dobie who was sitting bolt upright in a rocking chair by the window– 'Any chance of some food, ma'am,' he asked. 'I ain't ate since dawn.'

'Supper's at seven. I ain't gonna cook at any old time. Be here at seven and you'll eat, provided you ain't been drinkin' hard likker. If you drink – you don't eat here!'

'Not even if I've paid?'

'That's the rule, young man. Take it or leave it. What's your name?'

'Lee Masters, ma'am.'

Her eyes glittered– 'Related to Jeff Masters that owned the Circle M?'

'My brother, ma'am.'

Mrs Dobie snapped to her feet, fumbled in her dress and fairly flung Lee's two dollars back at him– 'I ain't havin' no Masters in my house!' she snapped. 'This here is a respectable house and I don't want none of your lot! Git!'

Lee picked up his money slowly– 'But, ma'am, I only just...'

'I don't care what you done or ain't done! I don't want none of your name here! Git!'

Lee shrugged, fetched his saddle and, watched by her hostile, beady eyes, tramped out; he went back to the livery stable whence Hughes had vanished, and hung his saddle on a peg in Black Powder's stall– 'Kinda unfriendly place we seem to struck, Powder,' he told the black, 'and seems like Jeff weren't too popular – in some quarters.' The big horse turned his head and blew gently into his master's face, then nipped at his vest pocket where, experience told him, he could expect to find sugar; Lee gave him some, patted his head and said– 'Awright for you, feller. But me, I ain't ate yet!'

However, he remedied that defect at a rough and ready sort of restaurant where the badly cooked food was served by a surly man who appeared interested in his customers' money and nothing else. As he drank his second cup of muddy coffee, Lee turned over in his mind what had happened since he had reached Lansing. It wasn't much but, such as it was, he didn't like it; whatever else she might be, Mrs Dobie had struck him as being rabidly honest and it was disturbing to discover that his brother had been the cause of such unreasoning detestation. It had been years since he had seen Jeff and he made himself recall as much as he could of his brother. Jeff had been big, strong, bossy, liking his own way and the good things of life, but – Lee asked himself – would Jeff have gone on the crook to obtain those good things? Lee thought not – and he thought objectively – his judgment unclouded by any love he had for his brother; Jeff hadn't been easy to get along with and Lee remembered him without overmuch affection, but he didn't think Jeff would do anything dishonest.

He stubbed out his fourth cigarette, got up and strolled out of the place– 'Guess it's maybe time I seen Cowin,' he told himself. 'Maybe he'll wise me up some. Now, where'd it say he hung out? Just beyond the saddlers and over the "Lulu" saloon.' He walked slowly down street, taking in the town as much as looking for the saddlers; to judge by the number of saloons, gambling joints and dance halls, it looked as though Lansing was the centre of a pretty busy cattle-raising area, and to judge by the names on the places of entertainment their proprietors had little initiative in the matter of titles.

The saddlers wasn't down street, so at the ragged edge of the town Lee turned back, walked nearly the full length before he found Hawkins saddlers shop, and in the alley between it and the 'Lulu' saloon and Dance Hall, an unsafe looking outside staircase which led up to a door which appeared as though it might have been painted within the last five years, and bore a wooden plate on which was scrawled– 'Ed Cowin. Attorney-at-Law'. Lee climbed the stairs carefully, the door opened at his touch and he paused at the entrance to a darkened room still thick with the smell of a burnt out oil lamp. Only when he had eased across the room to the window and released the roller blind was he able to see the room. It contained a rumpled truckle bed, a couple of chairs and a battered roll-top desk the contents of which appeared to have been scattered over the room as if by a tornado. Ed Cowin, once Attorney-at-Law, lay in a crumpled heap against one wall, where he had been flung by the impact of the double charge of buckshot which had almost blown him apart.

Lee Masters had seen death before, but there was something particularly unpleasant about that small, broken figure smashed so brutally against the wall of his shabby office. For a long moment he forgot his own problem and thought only of the dead man. The moment passed; Lee crossed swiftly to the door and closed it; if Cowin couldn't tell him anything perhaps the papers he had left behind would be more informative. Hampered by his inability to read quickly, Lee made as fast a search as he could; he had no wish to be discovered with the body, but apart from discovering that in the not so distant past Cowin had had a prosperous law business in Denver, he found nothing at all, no trace that his brother had ever been in to see the lawyer who had come down so far in the world.

Swearing softly, Lee eased out of the door– 'Guess I'll have to find the sheriff,' he muttered.

Outside the door his foot struck against something, something small; as he went down the steps he paused to pick it up; it was a drawn brass cartridge case which he examined quickly and slipped into his pocket; the gun which had fired it had a crooked striker pin for the mark on the base of the cartridge showed that the pin had very nearly missed the percussion cap– 'A clue?' he smiled wryly to himself. 'It could be. All I gotta do is find a shot-gun with a bent striker pin. Yeah! And there's scores of shotguns in this country I'll bet!'

Sheriff Barnes of Lansing County, looked far older than his fifty years; he was a dried-up, little man who looked as if the sun had sucked all the sap from his body and all the energy as well; his blue eyes were faded, his moustache drooped, and he sighed wearily as Lee finished his story– 'Cowin dead, huh?' he remarked. 'Pity. He hadn't been here long but he seemed a nice feller. Who'd want to kill him? Inoffensive cuss.' And here, somehow, the sheriff managed to suggest

23

that he also was an inoffensive cuss whom it was unfair to bother with such unpleasant matters as murder.

'Maybe the murderer was figgerin' to rob Cowin?' Lee suggested.

'Rob Cowin? He hadn't got two thin dimes to rub together! There ain't no law business in this town – folks mostly use a Colt. So you're Lee Masters, huh?'

'Yeah.'

'You look some like your brother.'

'Cowin wrote me he was dead.'

'Yeah, four or five weeks ago. Horse fell on him.'

'A horse? Jeff never fell off a bronc in his life!'

Barnes shrugged, his shoulders lifting so little it seemed he found even that much exertion exhausting– 'What they told me,' he said, 'he was forkin' a wild one.'

'But Jeff worked at horse-breakin' for years! Did you see him?'

'Me? Naw. It's quite a ways out to the Circle M, and – and I was all tied up with tax business.'

Lee stared at the Sheriff– 'You mean you never seen Jeff's body?'

Barnes moved uneasily in his chair– 'Was a couple of days afore I could git out – they'd planted him by then.'

Lee fished the makings out of his top pocket, rolled and lit a cigarette, he saw he wasn't going to get much out of Sheriff Barnes. As he drew smoke deep into his lungs he got to his feet– 'Wa'al, there it is, Sheriff. Cowin's been murdered. Guess you'd better git busy.'

'Busy? I ain't never anythin' but busy! If it ain't one thing it's another, always some dang trouble; dunno why I keep the job.' His voice trailed miserably away as Lee went out, swearing under his breath. Jeff killed by a horse? There was something mighty queer there Lee decided, for if there had been one thing Jeff had been able to do supremely well it had been to ride; and the Sheriff was clearly long past his job. Perhaps, once, he had been a good Law Officer; now it was all too clear that all he wanted was a quiet life.

Badly worried, Lee walked back to the 'Lulu' saloon which, he had noticed, looked reasonably clean from the outside; inside it was pretty clean too and, at that hour, almost deserted. One dark-haired, black-clad man sat at a poker table laying out a hand of solitaire; he flashed one keen, probing glance at Lee as the swing doors clashed behind him, then went back to his cards. Behind the bar a short, thick-set, pug-nosed barman smiled at Lee and asked cheerfully–

'What'll it be?'

Lee hooked a heel over the brass rail, grinned back and said– 'Schooner of beer,

25

and another smile; the first one seems kinda lonely in this town.'

'Stranger?' the barman asked, pouring the beer– 'I'm Ham – Fat Ham they mostly call me.'

Lee span a coin on the bar– 'You drinkin', Ham?'

'Sure, and thanks. I'll have a beer. Just hit town?'

'Kinda. Tried to fix me a room with Miz Dobie.'

'Tried?'

'Yeah. Got purty near thrown out when she found out my name is Lee Masters.'

'Any relation o' Jeff?'

'My brother. You know him?'

Ham's face hadn't lost its smile– 'Sure. Ain't many barmen in Lansing didn't. He sure was a free spender. You're a mite late for the funeral!'

'Yeah, I know. Had me a job in Tracy and didn't know Jeff was dead until the law-sharp wrote to me.'

'Cowin? Feller got our outside room?'

'Had. He's dead.'

'Dead? But I seen him last night!'

'Murdered. I found him and told the Sheriff.'

'Huh! Hell of a lot he'll do about it 'cept tell the undertaker. Murdered, you say? Hey! Brent! Old Ed Cowin's been murdered!'

The dark-haired gambler shuffled his

cards calmly together, stacked the pack neatly and came over to the bar; Lee noticed that he moved with the ease of a man who was supremely fit, that he had a wide pair of shoulders; Lee also noticed that a slight bulge under his left shoulder betrayed the presence of an under-arm gun– 'Name's Brent,' he said, his voice deep and pleasant. 'I own this joint.'

'Lee Masters.'

They gripped hands for a moment, their eye locked not exactly with hostility but with the neutral feeling that they would find it far from easy to get along– 'Cowin dead, huh?' Brent asked.

'Yeh. Blown apart with a shotgun. Musta been last night, the blind was drawn and the lamp had burnt out.'

'He was in here 'bout ten, Ham, wasn't he? I thought so. How come you found him, Masters?'

'He wrote me my brother was dead; I went to see him.'

'You the heir?'

'Cowin figgered so. How'd you guess?'

'No call for Cowin to write you otherwise.'

'You know Jeff?'

'Sure. He used my place some – not frequent, but some.'

'Know his wife?'

'Bella? Sure. Used to work for me. That's how Jeff met her.'

27

'Dance-hall gal, huh?'

Brent shrugged– 'Take a drink on the house, Masters.'

Ham poured, including himself in the invitation. Lee said– 'Luck! Brent, seein' you knew 'em both – well, could you say how come Jeff didn't will the ranch to his wife?'

Brent's eyes were inscrutable– 'Hard to tell,' he said. 'There has been talk as how they didn't git along, that Bella an' Benstead – the Circle M foreman – was too friendly, and then Bella's sister come out to live at the ranch. I dunno, Masters. I dunno. Jeff was a queer feller, used to have moods when he hadn't no use for anyone at all, he just naturally hated every dang person he knew. Guess he musta had one of them on him when he wrote his will. You seen it yet?'

'No I ain't. I figgered Cowin'd have it, but I couldn't find it.'

'Probably out at the ranch – if Bella ain't burnt it!'

Lee blinked– 'Would she have done that?'

'Wouldn't you if you was in her place? But Jeff might have left it at the Courthouse with Judge Purdy.'

'Purdy? Who's he?'

Brent's thin lips quirked in what was almost a sneer – 'Judge Purdy figgers to run this town,' he said, and from his tone of voice it was not difficult to deduce that there was no love lost between him and Purdy. 'Purdy had a big spread next to the Circle M,' Brent went on, 'and then reckoned he wanted to be a politician, stood for the State Legislature and didn't git no place, it made him so good and mad that he figgered he'd just run Lansing.'

'You say he had a big ranch?'

'Yeah – Diamond he brands, or his son does – Duke Purdy that is. He bosses the ranch now.'

'Where will I find this Purdy?'

'Courthouse I guess. He's mostly there when he ain't at Ma Dobie's; figgers he's Judge, Jury, and all.'

'Ain't nobody objected?'

'Someone did – once. They weren't alive to do it again. For all he's nearer sixty than fifty, Purdy pulls a fast gun himself and he's got fellers as do it for him too.' Brent's tone was bitter and Lee guessed there was something behind his dislike.

'How's he pay 'em?' Lee asked.

Brent shrugged– 'Ain't no secret,' he said. 'We gotta support our judge, me and the other saloon keepers, we have to pay taxes; Judge Purdy figgers drink is the root of all evil.'

'Like Ma Dobie?'

'You met her? Yeah, she's an old terror – she is. She'd have Lansing dry if she could but the Judge has got enough savvy to know that ain't sense. Feller comes in from a month on the range with his pay burnin' a hole in his pocket, he don't want to drink cawfee!'

Lee slid a five dollar bill across the counter – 'Drink up, gents.' He said. 'Seems to me like I'll need another couple of snorts 'fore I see this Judge Purdy feller.'

Chapter 3

Lee finally found Judge Purdy in his room at the Courthouse; it was a curious room, long, narrow, with the big desk behind which Purdy sat, at the far end from the door. Padded benches ran along either side wall, and above the Judge's head there hung a crude painting of George Washington under crossed flags and the legend 'E pluribus Unium'. The Judge himself was a big man verging on fatness, with a big face, a masterful chin and small, piercing eyes; he was, Lee decided, a hard man and quite possibly a bitter man–

'Who'n hell are you and what d'you want?' the Judge demanded. 'I'm busy!' However, since there was nothing on his desk there appeared little justification for his statement which merely served to annoy Lee who said–

'I'm Lee Masters. I've come to see you 'bout my brother's Will.'

At once there was the most extraordinary change in the Judge's heavy face on which a smile actually appeared – 'Why Jefferson Master's brother!' he said 'Yeh, there sure is a family likeness.' Lee's hand was wrung as Purdy surged up from his chair– 'Glad you've come to see me, young feller. I run this town and it's a right nice place for my friends. I'm sure we're gonna be friends!'

A little overwhelmed, Lee flexed his fingers– 'I went to see Cowin,' he explained. 'He wrote to me, but he's dead.'

'Yeh, so I heard – poor feller.' Judge Purdy might have been brushin a fly off his desk. 'Jeff had him draw his will up, and a right sensible will it was too.' He shook his massive head. 'That wife of his – he sure made a mistake when he married her, Jeff did, an' I told him so. Yes, sir! I sure told him. Still, he seen the light at last and kept the Circle M in the family.'

'I git it, huh?'

'Why sure you do. I seen Jeff's will. I witnessed it.' Under his bushy eyebrows Judge Purdy's sharp eyes stared aggressively at Lee; he appeared to be trying to convey the impression that he, and he alone, had persuaded Jeff to leave his ranch to his brother– 'Not only that, young feller,' he went on, 'but Jeff named me administrator too, means I gotta handle all the legal details and all, gettin' the will proved and such like things you wouldn't understand.'

'You mean I don't git the ranch yet?' To tell the truth Lee found himself in such a maze for the Judge spoke so fast and with so much assured authority–

''Course you got papers to sign,' Judge

Purdy went on. 'The law is kinda queer but we'll take care of that in good time. You just do as I advise you and things will be fine, just fine.'

'Y-yeah, I guess so. But I'd like to see the will. Have you got it, Judge?'

A shadow of annoyance passed over the Judge's florid face– 'You'll see it in good time, Lee,' he assured. 'Everythin's gonna be fine, just fine. Just do as I say. And now I got work to do so you just ramble. I know what you cow-punchers are – you like a drink or so. I don't but I'm not agin it.' He spoke with large generosity as if the whole State should be aware of and grateful for his tolerance. Lee submitted his hand to be wrung again, then he went out, still slightly dazed; he didn't see the speed with which the smile vanished from the Judge's face or the look of cold suspicion which at once replaced it.

Lee walked slowly out of the Courthouse, sat down upon the porch steps in the pleasant warmth of the sinking sun, rolled and lit a cigarette and considered his recent interview at his leisure while Lansing came to its evening life around him. For one thing he didn't trust Purdy, not one inch, quite apart from not liking the Judge's son; if Purdy had known of Cowin's murder he must have been told by the Sheriff who, in telling him, was bound to have mentioned who found the body. Yet Purdy had exhibited surprise at his arrival. Then there was the business of the will; Lee knew nothing of legal forms but the whole set up seemed queer to him and, queerest of all, just why the Judge should expect him to do as the Judge said– 'I'll be danged if I do,' he growled, pitched his cigarette butt away and walked back to the 'Lulu'. The place had filled up but Ham flashed him a smile–

'See the Judge?'

'Yeh, I seen him and I know what Brent means. Say, Ham, is there any place I kin git me a bed in this town? I got slung outa Ma Dobies on account of my name is Masters.'

'Sure, there's a spare bed where I room, back of the gunsmiths, up street a piece. Old Taylor'll let you have it; tell him I sent you and then stand back!'

Lee nodded his thanks, walked up street and found Taylor just shutting up his shop– 'Bed is it, huh? Thought you was gonna buy some guns, seein' the pair you're wearin' ain't new. Kin I look?'

Lee handed over his guns for the old man's inspection; he didn't like parting with them – even for a minute, but he needed a bed– 'Nice pair of weapons,' the old man said. 'Well balanced. I see you ain't marked 'em up with any of them dang fool notches! Used 'em much?'

'Not a lot,' Lee replied. 'They still throw straight.'

'If they're held straight!' the old gunsmith chuckled. 'There's a mort of fellers blame a gun when it ain't the gun's fault – and mostly it ain't. Yeah, you kin have the bed – and welcome. Got your bed-roll?'

'Left it at the livery stable. I'll git it.'

'See the bed first.'

The rooms behind the shop were clean and incredibly neat, the beds looked comfortable enough– 'Suits me,' Lee told the gunsmith. 'I'll go fetch my gear.'

On the way back from the livery stable, just as he came out from under the arch, bedroll over one shoulder– 'You Masters?' a rough, hard voice demanded.

Lee stopped, turned, his right thumb hooking itself into his gunbelt; the man who faced him looked like his voice, hard, bitter and dangerous– 'Yeah,' Lee said, 'what of it?'

'Judge Purdy wants you!'

In the fading light Lee could just make out that the man who'd stopped him was short, wiry, with cold eyes looking out from a still, cruel face; the man wore two guns, the bottoms of the holsters tied down– 'Right now,' Lee told him, 'I'm busy. And anyways, I just seen Judge Purdy.'

'He wants to see you agin, Masters, pronto! And when the Judge wants to see hombres – they go see him!'

Lee allowed the bedroll to slide off his left

shoulder, into the dust of the street– 'That so?' he answered mildly. 'Now ain't that somethin'? Every time the Judge calls they come a-runnin', huh? Wa'al, not me, feller. Like I said, I'm busy.'

The gunman stared at him, no trace of expression appearing on his immobile face; for a quarter of a minute he stared then he turned sharp on his heel and walked away towards the Courthouse; Lee shrugged, picked up his bedroll and went back to the gunsmith's. Old Taylor must have been watching, for as Lee climbed the steps to his boardwalk he asked– 'What's Harrison want?'

'Who's Harrison?'

'Feller that was talkin' to you.'

'Never seen him afore.'

'Be lucky if you don't see him agin. He's a killer. Works for the Judge. He's got a nice pair o' Colts, least they were till he filed the triggers.'

'Fans the hammer, huh?'

'Don't need to, the action's so light they pretty near jar off. I fixed 'em for him.'

'Works for the Judge, does he?'

'So folks say. Anyone Purdy wants killed, Harrison insults 'em into drawin' – then beats 'em to it.

'Legal murder, huh?'

'You said it, Masters, and I've said too much. Just forgit it, will you? What's Harrison want?'

36

'He said Purdy wanted to see me.'

'Then I'd go and see the Judge if I was you.'

'You ain't. And I ain't gonna chase after Purdy just on account he says so.'

'Suit yourself, son, but Purdy sure counts in this town.'

Lee shrugged as he dumped his bedroll– 'There ain't nobody gonna push me around,' he said. 'Comin' for a drink, Taylor?'

'Sure, I'd admire to. Let's go!'

The 'Lulu' had filled up considerably. Brent, from his place in a poker game, looked up as they came in and nodded briefly to Lee; behind the crowded bar Ham had time only for a quick grin and a– 'What'll it be, gents?'

As Lee sipped his whisky he noticed Brent call another man over, relinquish his place in the game and ease through the crowd– 'I heard you had a run in with Harrison, Masters?' he said, as he reached Lee.

'Run in? Hardly. He reckoned I had oughta to see Purdy. I didn't.'

'Harrison's dangerous.'

'So Taylor told me. So what?'

'So you ain't seen the last of him. Purdy don't give up easy. Harrison'll be back after you – here, and me, I don't like gun-play in my place. Mirrors come high.'

'Me, I won't be startin' nothin',' Lee said.

'Sure not. But it could be an idea to go

and see the Judge.'

'Me, I ain't takin' no orders from no one.'

'Suit yourself, feller. Here's Harrison now!'

In the flaring lamplight Harrison looked even less pleasant than he had appeared to be in the dusk; his face had the cold immobility of an alligator. He saw Lee at once – Lee knew, although he couldn't have told how for nothing showed in Harrison's pallid eyes.

Old Taylor sank his drink then shuffled to one side, his example at once followed by Brent and all the other customers who were anywhere near the possible line of fire. Harrison came forward slowly, his shoulders hunched a little forward, arms swinging so that the tips of his fingers brushed the walnut grips of his Colts– 'They purty near jar off,' Lee remembered Taylor saying, and for one horrible fraction of a second he was scared, scared of Harrison, scared of the smashing impact of a bullet, scared of death. But his fright passed as quickly as it had come; he had faced bad men before and knew that at heart most killers were cowards, dreading the day they would meet someone who drew more quickly, shot more straightly than they did, they knew it but yet had to do their own quarrel picking, forced on by the overwhelming fear of being thought afraid.

As Harrison moved away from the door,

not coming quite straight but a little to one side, another man came in, another gunman who sidled off the other side. Lee unhooked his boot heel from the bar rail as Harrison paused ten feet from him– 'I said the Judge wanted you, Masters!' his voice was low and bitter, but in the hushed silence of the bar-room it sounded loud.

'Wa'al, I'm here,' Lee told him. 'If the Judge is so all-fired eager to see me why don't he come his ownself 'stead of sendin' two cheap-skate dressed up gunmen?'

A sigh of suddenly released breath came from the audience at Lee's words; a faint flush crept up Harrison's neck – 'Kinda fancies himself, the Judge, don' he?' Lee went on. 'Havin' a couple of men to run his errands. He must think he's quite a feller, though speakin' personal I wouldn't have either of you runts go errands for me, not to fetch a dime's worth of tin-tacks!'

'Fill your hand, Masters, fill your hand!' Harrison couldn't quite keep the fury out of his voice just as he couldn't stop it glittering in his eyes; Lee's eyes were as much on the second gunman as they were on Harrison. Harrison, he thought, he had angered as much as he could – perhaps enough, he hoped, to make the gunman rush his draw–

'Fill my hand? Why? I got it filled right now, and with a right good glass of whisky! Here, taste it!' And with a twitch of his wrist he flung the contents, glass and all, at Harrison's face. Instinctively Harrison threw up a hand to guard his eyes, and while the glass was still in the air Lee, using the rail as a springboard, hurled himself in a low dive at Harrison's legs. As his shoulder hit Harrison's knees a gun crashed thunderously close to his ear, and then he was down on the floor, Harrison underneath him and fighting like a wildcat. Came another shot, further off this time, and splinters flew from the floor inches from Lee's face as he heaved himself up, kicked the gun from Harrison's hand and put a heel on the gunman's other wrist. One flashed glance told him the second gunman had ceased to be a problem; a tall, red-headed puncher had jumped him, wrapped long arms round him and was half-carrying, half-dragging him outside. Lee allowed himself a short, harsh bark of laughter, pulled Harrison's remaining gun away and tossed it out into the street, through the open door– 'Now git up, you polecat!' he ordered. 'You an' me are gonna talk!'

Harrison's eyes were fairly blazing with hate as he got slowly to his feet, he seemed slightly dazed for his hands fumbled at his empty holsters– 'I ain't tellin' you to fill your hands,' Lee said. 'I'm tellin' you to put 'em up!'

Harrison glared at him– 'Gimme my guns,' he snarled. 'I'll show you, you fourflushin'...' That was as far as he got before Lee's fist smashed into his face. Lee had no use for gunmen and from what Taylor had said he could guess just how much evil and misery had been caused by Harrison's skill with his gun. He set himself quite deliberately to smash Harrison, to do the maximum amount of damage without actually knocking him out. And a wreck Harrison was before one last smashing punch pulped his nose and sent him crashing back through the swing doors. Lee followed, gently rubbing his bruised knuckles, and watched while Harrison slowly gathered himself in the thick dust of the street; finally he lurched to his feet– 'Harrison,' Lee told him, 'when Purdy wants me, tell him to come and look for me his ownself!'

Harrison didn't answer, he just staggered away upstreet. Lee went back inside, found the tall, red-headed puncher who had dealt so expeditiously with the second gunman– 'Guess I owe you a drink, friend!' he said. 'I'm Lee Masters – and thanks!'

The red-head flushed until his face was redder than his hair– 'Shucks it weren't nothin'. Me, I don't admire to see no feller shot in the back.'

'What did you do with that jasper?'

'Threw his guns away and then threw him away – a long way!'

'Fine! What'll it be?' Lee moved back up to

41

the bar through a crowd that had only just begun to recover from its stunned amazement, a buzz of excited talk had succeeded the hushed silence and a number of men came forward to slap Lee on the back, to press congratulations and liquor on him. He knew exactly how little value was to be placed upon such a sudden admiring friendship, and turned the offers aside with as little offence as he could. Soon, he and the redhead found themselves more or less isolated at one end of the bar– 'Name's Lacy,' the redhead admitted. 'Franklin Lacy.'

'Stranger in town?'

'Yeh. Just got in.'

'Me too, though I reckon I been here long enough to find out that there wouldn't no citizen of Lansing helped me like you did; them two killers work for the jasper that thinks he owns the town.'

Lacy's wide mouth quirked in a grin– 'Speakin' personal I don't own the price of a drink, but this feller – whoever he is – ain't gonna own me. I'm glad I horned in.'

'Me too, Frank. That second feller would have got me else. You broke?'

'Flat. I need a job.'

'Could be you got one, Frank. Here's the set up...' And Lee told him what had happened. He liked the look of Franklin Lacy, quite apart from what he had done. Lacy's blue eyes looked straight at the world with an honest courage and he held himself like a man whose conscience was clear. He listened in silence to Lee's story and when it was done he said–

'I'm with you, Lee. Seems to me there's a powerful smell somewhere in this deal, and it seems to me too that you'll maybe be glad of someone who ain't been dippin' his spoon into the stew afore you got here. I'm hired. But this Purdy feller, how come he was so plumb friendly at first and then turned nasty?'

Lee said– 'My guess is he figgered I'd do just what he wanted, and turned tough when he found I wasn't gonna be so easy.'

'Could be. And could be he ain't done yet!'

'What you mean?'

'Wa'al, he's High Jack and Little Casino in this one-horse burg, and you busted him one on the snoot, didn't you? He ain't gonna like that, Purdy ain't. My guess is he ain't one to leave it where it is.'

'You mean he'll have another try?'

'Sure. And tonight, before it gits told around that he ain't the big feller he thought he was. I figger we oughta git outa town less'n we want to be shot at from around a corner.'

'You could be right, but...'

'I'll bet I'm right.'

'Where's yore horse?'

43

'Tied outside.'

'Mine's in the livery stable. We'll eat and then drift outa town. I ain't a coward but I ain't never admired to be dry-gulched. C'mon, let's ramble!'

Chapter 4

Franklyn Lacy had already made enquiries about getting a punching job and had, in the process, acquired some general idea of the position of the various ranches which used Lansing as their centre. Purdy's Diamond, the Box M, and a third ranch owned by a man called Wilkinson who branded Flying W, lay to the north of Lansing and were located in a valley running up into the Black Rock mountains. This valley, wide at the southern end towards Lansing, grew more and more narrow to the northward and, Lacy thought, the Box M was the furthest up the valley, with the Diamond to the West of it and the Flying W to the East. They got clear of town without any trouble; Lee left a short note for old Taylor, explaining that sudden urgent business had called him out of town.

They ate, with some care as regards unshaded windows, collected Lee's horse and left, riding hard as soon as they were past the last house, a rising moon giving them plenty of light. When the moon went down they pulled off the trail and slept for a few hours in the cover of the thick chaparral. Hungry again, they were up before dawn and riding towards the towering bulk of the Black Rock mountains. The well travelled trail was at first easy enough to follow, but when Lee reckoned they had made some fifteen miles from town it forked, one branch – and that the less used – going to the right– 'Flyin' W trail I'd guess,' Lee said. 'One that goes on should lead to the other two ranches. More traffic.'

'Sounds sense to me,' Lacy answered, and they pushed on. The mountains seemed close, so close it wasn't too easy to see the contours of the valley walls, but they had little doubt but that they were on the right trail. It was good range country by then, a change from the sandy, cactus strewn swales nearer town where even live oak and man-zanita had a hard task of existing; willows marked the windings of streams, there were cottonwood clumps and the grass was growing richer every mile. They also began to see cattle in pretty good shape, some branded Circle M and some – the majority, showing the Diamond. Two hours after dawn they saw the ranch buildings– 'Quite a spread you got, Lee!' Frank remarked when they were near enough to distinguish the details of the solid, well-kept ranch-house, the barns, corrals, bunk-house, wagon sheds.

'Yeah, quite some,' Lee agreed, 'but it sure is queer … Jeff, he never did like work much and all this... Hell! It's plumb hard to believe Jeff done the work that put this lot together. Why, it's the sort of spread for ten thousand head. Look at that bunkhouse! I'll bet that's got room for twenty men, Frank. Jeff sure musta changed.'

While they were still some distance away, half a dozen men emerged from the bunk-house, caught up their horses, saddled and rode away about their business, leaving a seventh man who walked towards the ranch-house. He was on his way back as Lee and Frank reached the bunk-house– 'Howdy!' he told them. 'Light and set down. Guess there's some chuck left.'

Lee swung down from his saddle, easing the soreness from his muscles–

'Quite a spread,' he commented to the stocky, wide-shouldered foreman.

'Yeah, but we ain't hirin',' the foreman answered. 'Sorry you had your ride for nothin'. Put your broncs up in the barn, there's plenty oats there. They'll need it after comin' out from town. You musta started plumb early!'

'Last night,' Lee told him, as Frank collected his black and led it away towards the stables. 'We slept out. Mrs Masters around?'

'Mis' Masters! Hell no, Mister! Why should she be?'

'But I thought...'

'You thought this was the Circle M?'

47

The foreman's face flushed with anger–
'By cripes not! This is the Diamond. Circle
M. Hell! That hole in the wall outfit?' He
was quite clearly furious at the very idea.

'Guess we musta been misdirected,' Lee
apologised. 'But seein' we're both strangers...'

'Sure. It ain't your fault,' the foreman
replied, 'you didn't mean nothin'. C'mon
in. Hey, Cookie! Nother couple o' customers! Hark at him swear,' he added under
his breath as the most illuminated burst of
language came from behind the serving
hatch at the end of the hall, followed almost
at once by the appearance of the cook's
furiously red face–

'Think I got nothin' better to do than
serve up meals to saddle tramps at any dang
time day or night?' he bawled. 'I got plenty
to do, I don't set and watch a stove you
know, Talon! I got to git the stuff ready! And
it takes time!'

'It's on'y a couple o' fellers that ain't had
no breakfast, cookie,' Talon pleaded, 'and
they come all the way from Tucson just on
account they heard you cooked so good!'

'Aargh!' The serving hatch came down
with a crash that shook the building,
followed by the clash of a pan on stove–
'You'll git food,' Talon promised. 'Cookie
likes his grouch, he does, but he kin cook.
Lookin' for a job, are you? Wa'al from what

48

I heard the Circle M ain't likely to be hirin'. It ain't a big spread, and the feller that owned it got himself killed by a bronc li'l while ago. My guess is the widder'll be sellin' – not hirin'.'

'Ain't much of a place, huh?' Lee queried.

Talon's eyes shuttled swiftly across Lee's face, a sharp, suspicious, probing glance strangely surprising coming from a man so apparently stolid and slow-witted– 'There ain't no love lost 'tween them and us,' he admitted. 'We reckon they brand mavericks and sleepers too dang prompt.'

'You sleeper much on this range?'

Talon shrugged– 'Brush up in the foothills is thick,' he explained. 'We don't aim to sleeper, but some git missed.'

At this point the cook dumped food through the service hatch; hot cakes, maple syrup, freshly fried steak and a pot of coffee, before reslamming the hatch with just as much emphasis as before– 'Git eatin',' Talon advised, 'and don' leave none or cookie'll blow up; he sure likes to see the food ate!'

The food was good, but there was so much of it they had to struggle to get through it– 'Boss come home last night,' Talon said, as Lee cut through his steak. 'Brung a wife with him and all. He's been down South buying breeding stock then come back sooner'n I expected on account there's a new railroad to Murray that saves three days on the ride from Tracy. Guess he figgered to catch me on the hop!'

Lee nodded and went on eating, hoping he would be able to get away from the Diamond without meeting either Duke Purdy or Laurel; he had arrived there as a result of a genuine mistake but he knew Purdy wouldn't believe that. As it happened his hope was vain, for as he waited outside the bunkhouse, talking idly to Talon while Frank got the horses, Purdy suddenly appeared round the corner, and stopped dead, his hand streaking to a gun– 'Masters!' he snapped. 'Did'n I tell you…?' Then he stopped at the sight of the Colt which had jumped into Lee's hand–

'I come here by mistake, Purdy,' Lee told him.

'Yeah? Now I'll tell one! I warned you not to come sneakin…'

'And I didn't.'

Then Laurel appeared behind Purdy. Lee felt himself flush as he dragged his hat off guiltily and holstered his gun – 'Why, Lee!' she said, also a little flushed. 'This is nice of you. I missed you at the wedding!'

'He ain't welcome here and he wouldn't have been welcome at the wedding. You keep outa this, Laurel. And you, Masters, climb your horse and ride.'

Lee noticed that Frank had already mounted and was watching closely, his hand near a gun butt, so he smiled at Laurel, gave her a sort of bow, put his hat back on and swung up into Black Powder's saddle– 'C'mon Frank,' he said, 'and thanks for the breakfast, Talon!'

As they turned their horses and rode away, Lee heard Purdy swearing at his foreman for having 'fed them two tramps'. And Talon gave back as good as he got, shouting that he wasn't going to have it told around that the Diamond wasn't hospitable.

Clear of the ranch they eased their horses to a lope– 'Looks like you were right about your brother not likin' work,' Frank suggested.

'Yeah, but I'll swear Jeff never turned crook.'

'Brandin' mavericks ain't crooked on some ranges.'

'On most it is, now that ranches have joint round-ups. Sure I know there's plenty of big spreads been built up with a runnin' iron, but them days are gone.'

They rode on in silence while Lee puzzled over the problems which faced him, trying to fit what had happened into some sort of pattern that could make sense; Cowin's letter, his murder, Judge Purdy's change of attitude; could that have been caused by some word he had received from his son? And where did Jeff's widow – Bella – come into it all? Was Brent, for whom Bella had worked, involved?

51

Lee wasn't much good at problems; after racking his brains for an hour he gave up and concentrated on following the trail to the Circle M, that Talon had indicated; from what Talon had told him they must have made their initial mistake when they'd chosen the wrong fork; the less travelled trail led to both Circle M and Flying W, dividing again five miles beyond the first branch. It was nearly noon before they reached the Circle M ranch buildings; these were built upon a low bluff which descended to a creek, a creek which came down from the neck of the valley. The ranch was well up the foot-hills, almost backed up against the steeper rising woods which reached to within a thousand feet or so of the summit; those last thousand feet were composed of bare, dark rock, the rock from which the mountain range took its name. The buildings them-selves fully justified Talon's description; ranch-house and bunk-house were one building, once no doubt stoutly constructed of properly chinked logs; now the roof sagged, several rotting timbers had not been replaced, doors and windows were crooked and unpainted, the whole place looked deserted and neglected. The single barn was in no better shape, and the moribund wagon shed held only a buckboard with a collapsed wheel, the corral posts leaned every which way and some of the rails were drooping as if ready to part company at the first touch.

All this they saw from half a mile away, saw at first glance before their attention was drawn away to the horse pasture which stretched between ranch and the fringe of underbrush which marked the beginning of the woods clothing the lower slopes of the mountains. There, a bay mare clearly enjoying herself was successfully eluding the efforts of a youth to catch her; the youth held his rope unskilfully and his casts were so inaccurate as to make Lee laugh loudly enough for the youth to hear; he turned, face flushing angrily, and Lee saw at once that the 'youth' was a girl, a slender, dark-haired, pretty girl whose grey eyes sparkled with annoyance– 'If you was gents,' she called, 'you'd come and help me rope this dang cayuse 'stead of settin' there laughin' your fool heads off.'

Lee swept his hat off his head– 'We sure will, ma'am,' he told her. 'Go catch it, Frank!'

Lacy clucked to his grey and the well-trained pony soon brought his master close enough to the mare for Frank's rope to reach. Lee watched, he wanted to see what sort of a hand with a rope Frank was. The answer – Frank was a top hand; he threw his rope with a quick, easy, flick of the wrist and the loop settled neatly over the mare's neck as she, seeing the rope, flung her head up; quite docile the mare allowed herself to be led back to the girl who had been trying to catch her– 'Ain't there no man aroun' to do this for you, Miss?' Frank asked, as he pulled his grey to a stop.

'The men on this ranch ain't fitter'n to be called rabbits, leave alone men!' the girl flashed at him. 'But thanks, stranger.'

'You aimin' to ride her?' Lee asked, noticing that the mare carried a Circle M brand.

'Who? Me? No, I was just gonna go fishin'! I was aimin' to use the mare for bait!'

Lee chuckled– 'I meant was you gonna use a saddle, Miss,' he said. 'Frank Lacy here would be plumb tickled to saddle up for you!'

She blushed faintly– 'Sorry I cracked wise, Mister,' she apologised 'and I'd sure admire for Mister Frank Lacy to saddle up for me. Seems there are gents in this country after all.'

Lee remembered that a sister of Jeff's widow had been mentioned, and he guessed that this girl who wore her levis as if well accustomed to them and had her hair bundled up under a Stetson, must be that sister– 'We'll go back to the ranch and fetch your saddle,' he said. 'Maybe you'd like to ride Black Powder – he ain't li'ble to explode!'

Her eyes sparkled– 'Gee! Ride that big horse! Hell, mister! I'd love to!'

Lee swung out of the saddle, almost laughing at the look of annoyance that appeared on Frank's face because he hadn't thought of it first. The girl went up into Black Powder's saddle like a squirrel, disdaining to make use of Lee's proffered hand. Black Powder didn't like it much, but at Lee's quiet word he decided to behave; Lee walked beside his head as they approached the ranch buildings which did not improve on closer inspection. No one appeared as they reached the hard packed earth space between the dilapidated dwelling quarters and the even more ruinous barn which, as Lee went in to find a saddle, he noticed smelled of decay– 'What a dump!' he muttered as he stumbled over a pile of rotting hay– 'Even worse'n Talon said!' He could only see one saddle, a big, heavy centre five with a high cantle which he swung down off its peg and carried outside– 'Where do you keep the blankets?' he asked the girl, to whom Black Powder seemed to have become accustomed already–

'Don't use 'em,' she replied.

'But hell! It ain't gonna do the bronc's back no good!'

'They're all so rotten and ragged they ain't much use.'

'I got two on my bronc,' Frank said. 'He don't really need both so you kin have one.'

The smile she flashed at him made him blush scarlet, and to cover his confusion he made a great to-do of unsaddling his horse and stripping off one blanket which Lee spread on the girl's mare before lifting the saddle up. As he tightened the single cinch the mare which until then had been quite docile, abruptly exploded; she pitched, bucked, sent Lee flying, and squealing with anger she hurled herself out of the yard. Lee sat up, scratched his head–

'Wa'al I'll be eternally danged!' he swore. 'What'n blazes happened?'

'Shore went on the prod sudden,' Frank said, re-saddling his own horse. 'In a hurry. I'll git her back.'

The girl slowly dismounted from Black Powder– 'That was Jeff's saddle,' she said in a hushed voice, 'and the horse that killed him acted the same way!'

'Did you see it?' Lee asked.

'No. At least not the end; the horse was known as a killer–Wilkinson sent it from the Flying W asking for Jeff to tame it.'

'And it killed him?'

'Yeah. He seemed to have it beat, rode slowly away to take the steam out of it and just as he was going away up the valley it started to act up worse'n ever. Did you know Jeff?'

'He was my brother,' Lee told her quietly.

'Then – then you're Lee! I'm April. Jeff married my sister Bella.'

'Howdy, April,' Lee grinned. ''Member me? We already met!' He looked into her eyes as their hands met, as he did so an image of Laurel seemed to flood between them and, to Lee's surprise, the recollection of the girl he had lost didn't seem to be nearly as bitter as it had been–

'Hey! I got the mare!' Frank interrupted them. 'She's sure on the prod!'

The mare was certainly in no sunny mood; she lashed out with all four feet as Lee approached her and the business of getting the saddle off her back was fraught with danger. However, he managed it in the end, and almost as soon as he had done so the mare quietened down, became docile once more and, after a while, allowed him to examine her back where he found that blood oozed from a small but deep prick. His face grim, Lee next turned his attention to the saddle, his fingers delicately feeling the underside; half a moment later, after some manipulation, he led up a long thorn–

'There's the trouble,' he said, 'and that didn't git there by accident.'

'What is it?' April queried.

'The Indians called it the "wait-awhile" thorn. See them barbs? You put it in somewhere there's movement, like the seams of a saddle, and it'll work its way in – and through.'

'You mean some'un put it in Jeff's saddle deliberately?'

'Musta done, it couldn't have got where I

57

found it by accident – and nor was Jeff's death an accident! Way I figger it, it sure looks like murder to me.'

Chapter 5

'Who'n blazes is talkin' about murder?'

Lee got slowly to his feet and turned to face the man who had come out of the house– 'And who the hell are you?' he asked belligerently. He was a short, broad-shouldered man, a rider by his clothes, but a toper to judge by the whisky flush on his nose and the three or four days' stubble of beard which bristled his chin– 'You keep outa this, gal,' he growled at April. 'Ain't I told you afore we don't want no strangers here?'

'And ain't I told you afore I ain't takin' no orders from you, you lousy Benstead?' she cracked back at him.

'Why, you little...!' So far he got before Frank's fist took him full in the mouth and he sat down with a bump. Lee was astonished at the speed with which Frank had moved. No slowcoach himself, he didn't think he could have been quicker–

'You'll take that back, Benstead,' Frank ordered quietly, and the hand he kept near a gun reinforced the command.

'Guess I spoke outa turn,' Benstead growled, after he had wiped his mouth with the back of his hand, looking at the smear of blood as if he'd never seen any before.

'Awright, git up then. Leave him be, Frank,' Lee said.

Frank stood back, still alert, and Benstead struggled to his feet.

'Who are you?' Lee demanded.

'Foreman,' Benstead answered sullenly.

'Hell of a foreman you are! You're fired!'

Utter astonishment showed in the man's bloodshot eyes, astonishment then anger – 'Fired? Whaddya mean? And who in Tophet you think you are, giving orders around here? Why I seen better things than you crawlin'!'

'Shut up!' Lee snapped. 'Pack your gear and ride! I want you offen my ranch in ten minutes!'

'Your ranch? Say, you got your nerve!'

'I'm Lee Masters!'

'Lee Masters!' Benstead breathed slowly, a cautious, cunning look on his face. 'Lee Masters!' Then his hand flashed to his Colt, lightning fast; but since Lee had hit the Lansing range he had learnt to be prepared for anything and he was not caught quite by surprise, his hand was only a fraction of a second behind Benstead's, his Colt was already swinging up as Benstead's belched flame; Lee felt the wind of the bullet as he pulled trigger. Benstead fired once more but, hit in the chest, his strength was already going and his Colt pointed to the ground; for a moment he stayed on his feet, then he collapsed like a busted flush. As he broke his Colt, pushed out the exploded cartridge and reloaded, Lee noticed that April had gone very white and he was just going to her when his attention was jerked away by a woman's voice saying– ''Bout time some'un took care of that big lug!' Out of the tail of his eye, Lee caught a glimpse of a look of amazement which replaced the horror on April's face, then he gave his full attention to the woman who leant against one of the porch poles, the woman who, he guessed, was his brother's widow.

Bella Masters wasn't at all like her sister except that both were dark-haired; Bella was taller, and built on much more ample lines, lines which were well displayed by the skin-tight dress she wore, a dress suitable enough for the 'Lulu' saloon and Dance Hall but utterly out of place at noon on a run-down ranch; she was also heavily made up.

Lee took his hat off– 'I'm Lee Masters, ma'am,' he told her.

'Yeah? You look a little like Jeff, but you act better. Jeff should have shot Benstead months ago.' She put up a hand to her carefully arranged hair and unleashed a smile at Lee that was so seductive it made him blush, and also tied his tongue. He noticed that Frank was staring at her in amazement, with his mouth wide open– 'Glad to know you, Lee,' she went on. 'I'm sure we'll be friends. Whyn't you come in? It sure is a pleasure to see a new face in this forsaken dump! There's some whisky too. Jeff growed him a corn patch, and for moonshine it ain't bad. C'mon in!'

'We'll have to do somethin' with Benstead, ma'am,' Lee protested.

'Bella, please!' she smiled. 'Seein' we're related there ain't no call to stand on ceremony, Lee.'

Lee felt himself blush again– 'Any other hands on the ranch, ma'am?' he asked.

'Yeah, one or two – I forget. There were more but they didn't git paid so they quit.'

'The two that are left are out ridin',' April told him. 'Benstead sent them to mend a fence up at the canyon, they'll not be back before dark.' The glance she shot at Bella could hardly have been more unsisterly, and it was pretty clear that she had her own ideas of the reason why Benstead had wished to be the only man at the ranch-house–

'We'll plant him first an' talk after, ma'am,' Lee told her curtly. 'Where will I find a pick an' shovel?'

Bella shrugged– 'I wouldn't know,' she said, and flounced back into the ranch-house; it was April who found them the tools with which to carry out the unpleasant task, April who showed them where Jeff Masters had been buried, after which she vanished.

The ground was pretty hard and rocky and they were sweating freely before the grave was deep enough– 'He shore slung a fast gun,' Frank said as they carried the body out of the yard.

'Yeah, I almost got mine; I felt the bullet.'

'Queer set-up, ain't it?'

'Gits queerer and queerer. Some'un told me that Jeff's widow and the foreman…'

'Looks like that all wore out?'

'Yeah. Ease him over a bit, Frank, I'm gonna search him.'

Lee hadn't any real expectation of finding anything, and at first the search yielded only such things as he expected, a letter, cash, tobacco, matches, odd bits of twine, a broken spur and all the raffle of useless stuff an untidy man allows to accumulate in his pockets. Only when he reached inside Benstead's tobacco sack did he find the note– 'Masters is in town,' it said, 'so watch out!' Its only signature was a squiggle which could have been almost anything but looked less unlike a 'B' than any other. 'Now who'n hell would think it worth while to send this all the way from town?' Lee puzzled.

'Musta been a good reason,' Frank replied. 'It's nearer thirty than twenty miles.'

'I know. And I only hit town yesterday so Benstead couldn't have had it long!'

'And soon's he finds out who you are he

goes for a gun!'

'Yeah, but he was good and mad by then. There's somethin' crooked back of all this, Frank, I'll just nacherly swear there is, just as I'll swear Jeff hadn't nothin' to do with it.'

'I wouldn't say the same for his wife.' Frank commented, as he shovelled earth over Benstead.

'Me neither. That's another thing I just don't understand; she's nothin' but a honky-tonk gal, and Jeff, he never had much use for 'em!'

'Long time no see. He could have changed, Lee.'

'Aw, sure. Wa'al, that's him planted.' He got to his feet and stood looking down at the low mound which covered his brother's body– 'I'd sure like to know about you, Jeff,' he muttered.

'You still figger that horse couldn't have killed him?'

'Hell! I dunno. With that thorn stickin' in him almost any old hay-burner could have went good an' mad. But Jeff, he sure could ride.'

Frank leant on his shovel– 'Wanta take a look?' he asked quietly.

'I dunno. I just don't know, Frank. I'd like to, but it don't seem right to disturb him. I reckon Jeff was murdered; the how of it don't matter too much, I guess. S'pose I'd better go and talk to this Bella. You comin'?'

64

'Reckon not. I'll take me a li'l ride, have me a look at the cattle.'

'And April?' Lee said with a smile.

Frank blushed– 'I dunno which way she went.'

'That mare would have left tracks!' Lee reminded him.

Chapter 6

The moonshine Jeff Masters had made was pretty rough, his first sip made Lee gasp as the liquid fire trickled down to his stomach; the parlour of the ranch-house was in little better condition than the outside, the furniture was old and battered, the plank floor dirty and rotted in some places, some of the chairs were littered with grubby items of feminine attire. Bella lounged seductively on a sagging couch, the moonshine jug on a table beside her; the glass she'd poured for herself when she gave Lee one, hadn't been her first– 'Sure is nice to see you, Lee,' she told him, her voice just the merest trifle thick– 'Nice of you to come. You gonna help me run the ranch?'

He took another sip of the firewater to give himself a little more time to try to think out how he was going to approach the subject which had been on his mind ever since he'd first seen her– 'You – you reckon it's your ranch?' he blurted out at last, unable to imagine any way in which to wrap up the question that had to be asked.

'My ranch? 'Course it is! Why shouldn't it be? I'm Jeff's widow, ain't I?'

'Yeah sure, but Jeff willed the ranch to me!' There, it was out, the cat was out of the bag, and it wasn't a cat at all but a full-grown mountain lion. For two or three seconds Bella stared at him, all seduction gone from her eyes leaving them hard, predatory, bitter and grasping as her mouth which had suddenly become as uninviting as a rat-trap—

'He willed the ranch to you? I don't believe it!'

'True enough. Ed Cowin, he told me so!'

'Cowin? That cheap-skate lawsharp! He's dead anyway!'

Lee knew from that remark that the man who had brought the note out to Benstead had brought news as well – or had the note been sent to Bella and passed on by her to the foreman?

'Yeah, he's dead – murdered,' Lee said. 'But Judge Purdy told me about the ranch.'

'That pompous old windbag! Where's the will? I ain't believin' this till I seen it – though it could be just the lousy, two-timin' sort of trick that psalm-singin', Bible-punchin' swine – Jeff Masters would play on me. Turn me outa my home, would he? And you, you thievin' scum! You think I'm gonna pack my traps and leave just on your say-so? Hell no, mister! I ain't no dumb hick. I been around! I ain't fallin' for no story like that! Show me the will and I'll believe it, Masters, otherwise drift, feller! Drift!'

67

Lee smiled at her; he was almost relieved that she had so quickly shown herself in her true colours; if she had been tearful, pleading, he would have felt dreadful about it, but now there was no need for that– 'Jeff willed me the ranch,' he told her firmly. 'I ain't got the will now, but I soon shall have. I ain't askin' you to leave pronto – it's only right you should have time to make arrangements.'

'Only right! You're just like Jeff – allus the li'l gent, ain't you? I'm plumb sick of the lot of you. This is my ranch and I'm stickin'! And as for you – take that!'

Lee easily avoided the cup she threw at his head, and escaped quickly from the room; as he went through the door he saw her lift the moonshine jug, but as he heard no crash he assumed she'd lifted it to drink and not to throw.

Outside, he drew a deep breath, sat down upon the porch to roll a cigarette and try to sort out this thoughts; his efforts, however, were interrupted by a strange voice saying– 'Quite a piece, ain't she?'

Recent events made his hand jump towards a gun as he looked round, but he pulled his hand away in some embarrassment when he saw the bent, little, old man who had addressed him. Bent and old the man might be but there was a friendly gleam in his still bright eyes and Lee gave him a grin– 'Quite a piece,' he agreed.

'You Jeff's brother? I should have guessed it anyway even if...'

'Even if you hadn't listened?' Lee finished.

'Yeah, I listened. Get to be as old as I am and you'll find folks don't tell you nothin' no more so you gotta find out for yourself. Jeff willed you the ranch, huh?'

'Danged if I know, Pa,' Lee answered, pushing his hat to the back of his head and abusing his hair. 'I just dunno. Me and Jeff never did git along too good, and I gotta admit I was plumb astonished when I heard Jeff had willed me his ranch.'

'Maybe you was astonished, but I'll bet you wasn't so dang mad as her!' He jerked his thumb towards the window. 'I heard,' he chuckled, 'I heard Jeff tell her he wasn't gonna have her git the ranch.'

Lee sat up– 'What'n hell do you mean?' He demanded. 'Did Jeff know he was gonna die?'

'Not as far as I know. But she was allus on at him to make a will. Here, I got cawfee perkin' back on the stove. C'mon and drink some.' The old fellow led the way round the back of the bunk-house part of the building to a lean-to cook shack. Inside, was neat as a new pin, clean, shining– 'I like things neat,' he explained, 'won't have that slut in my place, not for nothin'. I'm the cook here,' the old man explained, 'and mostly everybody

69

calls me Pa. I been called Pa so long I 'most forgot my name – which same don't matter none anyway.' He looked keenly at Lee– 'I – I kinda go with the ranch,' he stated, 'and if it's yourn...'

Lee smiled– 'I'll need a cook,' he replied.

'Fine! Y'see,' Pa went on as he fetched the coffee, 'I been here a right many years. Yeah, I seen three owners and I'm gettin' kinda old to move.'

'How long did Jeff have the place?'

''Bout a couple of years. He won it in a poker game. It weren't so run-down then, though it had begun to slide.'

Lee sighed; he hadn't been so far wrong about Jeff not liking work; to win a ranch in a gamble was the only way Jeff could have gotten one– 'And her?' he asked, jerking his thumb towards the other end of the building– 'did he win her in a poker game, or find her under a holly bush?'

Pa used a splinter to extract coffee grounds from between his teeth– 'I dunno about her,' he said. 'Jeff never struck me as the marryin' kind – and I seen some. One day he come back from town with her on a livery horse – just like that. Said they'd gotten married the day before, and it weren't the day after they was fightin' to beat creation!'

'Then why in hell did they git married?'

'Now that I wouldn't be knowin'; though Jeff had a powerful hangover on him the next day and I did hear tell, in a roundabout way you'll understand, that some folks were sayin' she wouldn't be sorry to find a husband. Even in Lansing some of the wives reckon they're respectable, and so it is said, that some of the things Bella did were darin' even for a dance-hall gal; there was talk of her bein' rid outa town on a rail, and tarred and feathered and sich like. And now I have somethin' for ye, Lee Masters,' the old cook went on. 'Your brother trusted me – as well he might! And he left me a letter to give you when you arrived.'

The old man lifted a plank of the table and there, stuck to the underside of it, was a thin package addressed to Lee in what he recognised as his brother's awkward writing. There wasn't much of it, and after he'd laboriously spelled it out twice, while he had the answer to some questions Lee had some new ones to cause him further punishment–
'I'm sorry we weren't better friends,' Jeff had written, 'and I figgered it was mostly my fault, and I'm sorry we won't meet so that I can tell you. But we won't, because I'll be dead soon. And, Lee, however I die – I'll have been murdered. They wouldn't stand for my backing out – but I can't help that; I can't go on crooked, not after what happened last month and I won't tell them what they want to know. I'm telling you, Lee, and I'm telling you this way because although I

think Pa is straight, I'm not all that certain. You remember Owl Canyon where we used to play? I guess you do because you'll be reminded of it by a bit of this ranch; if you remember that you'll remember where we hid that old shot-gun Dad said we mustn't use. That's it, Lee, all you need to know. You can guess the rest. Now about the ranch – I want you to have it. I came by it fairly straight for me; won it in a poker game. I was cheating but the feller I won it from had cheated me plenty. Bella saw me cheat – that's why I had to marry her, to keep her mouth shut – the bitch. I've made a will too. Ed Cowin's got that and will tell you when I'm killed. I had Judge Purdy witness it so you shouldn't have no trouble that way. That's all, Lee – and good luck!'

As Lee, his mind in a turmoil of speculation, folded the note preparatory to putting it away in his pocket, the cook-shack door flew open and a voice that was meant to be hearty but failed by quite a lot said– 'Wa'al, wa'al! Chinnin' with the cook, huh? You must be Lee Masters? I'd sure know you anywheres! Dan Wilkinson's my name, and mighty glad to meet my dear friend Jeff's brother. Put it there!'

Lee put it 'there' with some reluctance as he got up from behind the table. Wilkinson was dark, a man of medium height, carefully dressed in range clothes that were all dark and nearly new; he wore two guns, and a thin moustache smeared his upper lip. Lee knew, that he had seen Jeff's note, he also realised that Wilkinson knew he knew, and that he guessed Wilkinson knew who wrote it; for one moment Wilkinson's dark eyes had been very expressive– 'I'm just findin' out about the ranch,' Lee explained lamely. 'Maybe you'd like some cawfee?'

'Cawfee? That's a laugh! Not for me, friend – me for the jug! I helped Jeff make the last li'l lot and it should be gittin' to be good. We'll go see Bella – and hope she ain't drunk it all!'

Laughing too much at his own joke, he took Lee's arm and hustled rather than helped him out of the cook-shack; as he left, Lee took one look at Pa – and if ever he saw hate in a man's eyes he saw it in Pa's, the old man would obviously have liked nothing better than to stick a knife into Wilkinson–

'Never seen this section before?' Wilkinson asked, as he and Lee walked round the building. Lee had shaken his arm free – and none too gently at that– 'Yeah, first time here,' he agreed.

'Fine country,' Wilkinson went on. 'Good feed, good water, not too far to drive. Only trouble is rustlers!'

'Rustlers?' Lee queried. 'First I heard of 'em.'

'Ain't surprisin',' Wilkinson told him.

'Purdy's lost quite some cows; Jeff lost plenty; and me, I don't know what my owners'll say when they see my tally sheets.'

'Your owners? Why, I heard...'

'Heard I owned the Flyin' W? It ain't so. It's just a coincidence my name beginnin' with a "W". I'm Manager – and that's all. Welland Cattle Company own the spread, and they ain't gonna like the number of cows I been losin'. Here's the house. Hi, Bella!'

'Whyn't you come'n see me first, Ed? You lousy skunk!' Bella's voice had thickened up quite some and as she came out of the door she swayed and had to grab at the porch to keep upright, but she gave Wilkinson the same incredibly seductive smile she gave Lee–

'Hadda go and see Jeff's brother,' Wilkinson told her. 'And ain't he like Jeff?'

'Yeah, just the same sort of measly, psalm-singin' lughead!' she exclaimed. 'What you want, Ed?'

'Right now I could do with a small snort of that moonshine.'

She leered at him– 'And is that all you come for?' she asked.

'Come to see your purty eyes, Bella, and have a chat with the new owner of the Circle M.'

'And that's me, too!' she bawled. 'Don't let anyone tell you different, Ed Wilkinson. I own the spread and I'm gonna run it!'

'In a pig's ear!' Wilkinson pulled her up. 'Shut your yap, Bella! You couldn't run a ten-yard race! And it ain't your ranch, Jeff left it to his brother!'

'Why you...' Oaths came in a stream from her painted lips, oaths she backed up with violence or attempted violence; she went for Wilkinson like a wildcat, kicking and scratching. Wilkinson tried to beat her off but she was a big, powerful woman and he didn't have much success until Lee wrapped his arm round her and swung her off her feet and then carried her inside the ranch-house. For a minute or two she still fought furiously, almost insanely; then, with a suddenness that caught Lee by surprise, she went limp and slid out of his arms, in another moment her arms were round his neck, her body pressed hard against his, while her lips sought hungrily for his– 'Ain't nobody carried me like that for years,' she whispered. 'Hold me tight, honey! Tight! You won't hurt me.'

'Well!' April's quiet voice commented from the door. 'Well, you two certainly got friendly!'

Lee, furiously angry, tried to release himself from Bella's clinging grasp; he was acutely aware that in her struggle with Wilkinson her dress had suffered severely and she was by that time, whether by accident or design, not so very far from being naked. Bella was a woman who had plenty to show and didn't mind showing it. Without letting go of Lee, she turned her head to look at her sister– 'Scat, kid!' she ordered. 'Me and Lee are busy!'

'We ain't,' Lee growled, and at last succeeded in breaking from the grip of her arms around his neck; but April had gone, leaving Lee strangely angry with himself for allowing himself to be caught in such a situation.

Wilkinson strolled in, a leering smile on his face– 'Made it up, huh? You sure work fast, Lee! Just about as fast as Jeff did. And, Bella, maybe you don't feel it but that dress sure looks draughty!'

Almost of their own accord Lee's hands leapt to his guns; in one flashing instant Wilkinson's astonished eyes were presented with the gaping muzzles of two Colts– 'Out!' Lee ordered. 'Grab your bronc and ride!'

'But hell, Masters! We're gonna be friends! We're gonna be neighbours now you own the Circle M!'

'He owns the Circle M?' Bella yelped. 'Hell he does! I own it, Ed, I'm Jeff's widow and it comes to me!'

'Not when he willed it to his brother,' Wilkinson told her.

'But that's crazy! The law can't allow a

man to leave his wife without a cent!'

'It sure can, Bella. You got the will ain't you, Lee?'

Lee slowly re-holstered his Colts; it had been automatic for him to resent an insult to a woman, but since Bella had, for one thing, shown she could take care of herself, and for another seemed completely unconcerned by her near nakedness, he didn't see why he should worry–

'No, I ain't got the will yet,' he said.

'Then you don't own the spread,' Bella told him curtly. 'So you kin git, same's you told Ed to!' Her mood had veered round again and now she was as hostile as before she had been seductive.

'Yeah, but it will be his, Bella,' Wilkinson pointed out in a voice meant to be reasonable. 'The law's gonna uphold that will when it's found.'

'Until then the Circle M's mine!' she declared.

'You got the money to pay wages, and food, and such like?' Lee queried.

'Ought to be plenty in the Bank.'

'Jeff's money? They won't let you touch it.'

'Why not? I'm his widow! I gotta live.'

'Banks don't care about that,' Wilkinson told her curtly. 'They'll pay the money to Lee when he shows them the will.'

'And meanwhile I kin starve?'

'Sure! Maybe you ain't so clever as you

thought you was, Bella. Maybe you should have treated Jeff at least part-way decent!'

In a flash she was at him again, perhaps even more violently than before, but this time Wilkinson didn't stand any nonsense, he met her with a crisp right to the chin which knocked her out– 'Don't like doin' that to a woman,' he said, as he and Lee laid her on the couch, 'but sometimes there ain't nothin' else to do. She led Jeff a dawg's life, can't understand why'n hell he married her. Course it ain't none of my business but I'd heave her and her sister out – pronto.'

'Reckon I won't do that,' Lee said. 'Not pronto anyhow; they got to live someplace.'

'Suit yourself. Me, I wouldn't live within a mile of that hell-cat. And the sister's got the hell of a temper too. Wa'al, so long, Lee. Sorry if I spoke outa turn, but you know how it is now. Lemme know if you need any help; I kin spare a couple of hands for a few days.'

Chapter 7

That night Lee lay in his bunk for a long time before sleep came, his brain too busy reviewing the events of the day, to relax. He and Bella had come to some sort of agreement that she and April would stay at the ranch until the will was proved, and meanwhile Lee would take care of the current expenses. If the will wasn't found, or turned out to be in Bella's favour Lee would cut his losses and leave; he had a few hundred dollars saved up and from what he had seen of the ranch he knew it could, with proper handling, be made a paying proposition. At the moment it was anything but that, for when the two elderly Circle M punchers returned at dusk their report on the Circle M stock wasn't encouraging; apparently Jeff had, up to some few months before, been dribbling his saleable cattle away in penny packets, selling a dozen steers to pay a feed bill, losing four or five in a poker game; that process, they told him, had stopped, but it had made serious inroads on the cattle available for a beef cut and he found fresh worry in the very fact that it had stopped. In his letter Jeff had admitted he had been involved in something crooked, and in cattle country, apart from robbing a bank or holding up a stage, rustling was one of the few remaining illegal undertakings, and Wilkinson had said there was rustling on the Lansing range. Lee couldn't help but come to the reluctant conclusion that his brother had been a rustler; equally, he was convinced that Jeff hadn't been alone in it. Rustling anyway, unless he was merely putting his own brand on some of his neighbour's cows, wasn't a one-man job; to make sufficient out of it to be able to stop selling his beef cattle, he argued that Jeff must have been in it on a fairly large scale. From what he had seen of Schultz and Murphy – the two Circle M punchers – Lee was sure that whoever had been in it with Jeff, it hadn't been them; both were getting on in years, both appeared to be of slightly lower than average intelligence; if they had been in it with Jeff they would never have had the sense to quit when he had and it was clear that his death had been the result of his having quit. Which brought Lee to the thing that had puzzled him most in his brother's letter, Jeff's reference to their boyhood games in Owl Canyon; Lee remembered it only vaguely, he had been the younger by some years when they'd played there, but from that dim remembrance he could conjure up no image bearing a resemblance to anything he had seen thus far on the Circle M range.

His tired brain at last gave up the struggle and he drifted off into a dream-disturbed sleep from which he was roused by Pa vigorously hammering on a frying pan.

Supper the night before hadn't been generous; breakfast was even less adequate– 'I can't cook what I ain't got,' Pa explained grumpily when Lee asked him about it. 'I ain't got no eggs, dang little flour, and I'm outa bacon.'

Lee smiled at Frank– 'Care for a ride to town?' he asked.

'Yeh, sure,' Frank replied.

'Fine. Then all we gotta do is fix that buckboard.'

'That one with the crumpled wheel?'

'Got it in one!'

Frank groaned– 'But we'll need a new wheel!'

'I guess the boss is maybe usable,' Lee encouraged him. He sent Schultz and Murphy back to their fence mending, told them he would fetch more wire to replenish the almost vanished stock and then he and Frank set about mending the buckboard; April appeared, helped them find the tools they needed – or as many as were available, all of which were in a poor state. They found the rim and boss of the wheel were just usable but they fashioned new spokes all round; when they'd assembled the wheel there was the tyre to be shrunk on, and before they could heat it they found they had to mend the forge bellows– 'Allus some dang thing,' Frank grumbled, as he tacked a new piece of leather on the bellows, ''pears like this whole dang ranch is held together by a piece of string!'

'Yeah,' April agreed. She had appointed herself a sort of carpenter's mate to Frank and, for some reason he couldn't fathom, this annoyed Lee intensely– 'Yeah,' she said, 'and me, I'm glad I'm leavin'.'

Frank sank back on his heels and looked up at her– 'Why?' he asked bluntly.

'Oh I'm well again now, and I'm going back to teaching school in Tucson; I only came out because I'd been ill, an' Bella said her husband had a ranch. Now she ain't got a husband – or a ranch, I'm not gonna be a burden to her.'

'Shucks! You couldn't be that to no one,' Frank told her warmly, and once again Lee felt an unaccountable twinge of annoyance because he hadn't said it first–

'If it was my ranch, Miss April, you'd sure be welcome to stay,' Lee said, uneasily aware that he wasn't speaking as comfortably as he meant to.

'Sure is nice of you, Mister Masters, but I got myself to keep and I ain't taking charity from no one.'

'It ain't charity,' Lee answered hotly, and

then stopped, realising that if April did stay on it would be under conditions so like charity as to be almost indistinguishable.

'Kin I ride to town in the buckboard with you?' she asked.

'Why sure,' Lee replied, glad she had changed the subject, 'but it won't be today; we'll have to make an early start tomorrow if we're gonna git back afore dark. Are there any buckboard plugs on the ranch?'

'Well, there was a pair that Jeff used once – when he fetched me, but he broke the wheel not long after and they haven't been used since. They were good and wild then!'

'I better see what they're like. You finish the wheel, Frank. And, April, could you point out them plugs to me?' As they walked away Lee looked back and grinned at Frank whose gesture, in reply, was anything but respectful.

In the pasture April pointed out a couple of wiry mustangs; they still showed faint marks of saddle harness but as she had warned – they were good and wild. Lee saddled up Black Powder, roped the pair easily enough but he had a struggle to get harness on them. When he had, at length, managed that, he secured the harness traces to a heavy baulk of timber and let the mustangs work off some steam in dragging that over the rough ground; after an hour at that they were more meek and mild and didn't try to argue much when Lee put them to the rejuvenated buckboard, they even stood quiet for a moment or two before he let them feel the whip; then they did indeed try to catch the sun, but Lee held them firmly and took the rest of the steam out of them in a five mile gallop out and back along the trail.

The mustangs were fresh as paint again by the morning so made nothing of the buckboard load of April, Frank and Lee, both of whom noticed, without comment, that April had brought no box of her belongings and said nothing further about leaving the Circle M. The buckboard rolled into town more than two hours before noon; the mustangs – running steadily, having covered the thirty miles in under three hours. Lee put them up at Hughes livery stable, baited them generously before he left them– 'Where to?' Frank queried.

'"The Lulu",' Lee said shortly, 'or rather Cowin's room above it.'

'If you two are gonna drink...' April's voice was sharp, 'I'm going to visit with Mrs Thomas, her husband keeps the store and she sent word she's some more ginghams in she wanted me to see.' With that she turned and swept off with as much dignity about her small, slender figure as if she'd been a congressman's wife.

Lee chuckled as he watched her go– 'Sure

got her nerve!' he said, 'but she'll do to take along.'

'Yeah,' Frank agreed shortly. 'Lulu?'

Lee lifted an eyebrow, shrugged, and they walked to the saloon in a silence which while not hostile, was hardly friendly; again Lee was mildly surprised at his feelings, he still regarded himself as hopelessly in love with Laurel, yet when he came to try he found it quite difficult to call up any very vivid recollection of her face; April's pert little nose kept getting in the way.

The 'Lulu', at that time of day, was deserted apart from a swamper wielding a lazy broom among the chairs and tables, and Ham polishing glasses behind the bar–'Mite early,' he commented, 'but I reckon I need one!' He slid glasses across the counter to them, and followed up with a bottle–'Find your ranch?' he asked.

Lee filled his glass– 'I found it,' he said. 'Luck!'

Ham nodded– 'Not so good, eh? I did hear Jeff had let it run down.'

'Musta been on the skids afore he got it. He just let it go on slidin'. Set 'em up again, Ham. And tell me, you said Jeff used to come in here sometimes? He have any particular friends?'

Ham's glance was shrewd as he bent to pick up his polishing cloth– 'Jeff used to work for the Diamond,' he said, ''fore he won the Circle M offen Mitchell who had it afore; Jeff and Wilkinson were thick once, lately they fell out – or so it seemed to me.'

'And Brent? Were him and Jeff thick?'

'Now you're askin' 'bout my boss, Masters.'

'Yeh, awright, Ham. Say, I wanta to have a look at Ed Cowin's room. Anyone usin' it?'

'Not as far as I know. Sheriff took Ed away day 'fore yesterday – we planted him yesterday. I'll go and ask the boss!' He went away, came back after an interval with Brent who didn't look too pleased at being disturbed–

'You wanta see Cowin's room, Masters? Why?'

'I ain't found Jeff's will yet,' Lee said, 'and I need it. Cowin was Jeff's Attorney and it could be the will is up in his room.'

Brent scratched his unshaven chin– 'Wa'al, I dunno,' he said. 'I guess there's legal difficulties. Cowin's stuff must belong to some'un. I dunno...'

'I'd sure be obliged,' Lee said, suddenly annoyed that he should have to plead with Brent.

Brent yielded– 'Awright,' he replied, 'but I better come with you, I don't want no trouble.'

Some attempt had been made to clear up the mess in Cowin's room but it hadn't been a very good try, the papers which, before, had been scattered were now scooped together in a heap, and that was about all.

Brent settled himself into the rocking chair and said sourly– 'Wa'al, git looking!'

Lee put his hands on his hips and looked the room over carefully, trying to think of some place where Cowin might have concealed the will which, for some reason Lee couldn't understand, had to be hidden. While Frank Lacy took the still crumpled bed apart, Lee made for the desk, he pulled all the drawers out and looked underneath them, remembering where Jeff's letter to him had been concealed; he sounded and measured for secret compartments but without any luck. Brent lit a cigar and smoked steadily without offering either help or suggestions. Baffled by the desk, Lee tried the floor; again no luck, all the boards were solid and surprisingly close fitted, no room to get even a cigarette paper between them. Once more out of luck he got back on his feet, swearing under his breath; he again stared round the room, with impressions of failure growing in his mind. Frank had drawn a blank with the bed and now squatted on his heels, going through a pile of papers, the speed with which he did it showing that he could read with greater facility than Lee who was somewhat annoyed by this demonstration of his hired hand's superior education– 'There ain't nothin' here,' Frank said, throwing down the last paper. 'Who'n hell was this Cowin anyway?'

Brent pointed to the glass-framed certificate which hung over the desk; it stated that Edward Charles Cowin was licensed to practise law in the state of Iowa. 'My guess is he was on the dodge,' Brent said. 'I know he practised in Denver and had to leave there on the jump, but I never noticed afore that he come from Iowa.'

'Here! Let's have a look at that,' Lee said, sudden hope lighting his gloom as he took the certificate frame down from the wall; he turned it over and noticed that the back appeared to have been glued more recently than the rest; he tore away the cardboard and out fell a folded sheet of paper; before Lee could reach down to it Brent leant forward and snatched it up–

'It's the will awright,' he said, 'and he's left his ranch to you, Masters!'

'Thanks, Brent,' Lee said quietly. 'I'll take it.'

'No, no! I think not,' Brent answered, and for the first time Lee noticed that he had a gun in his hand–

'What'n hell are you playin' at, Brent?' Lee demanded. 'This ain't none of your put in. Gimme that will!'

'No!' Brent repeated. He got carefully out of his chair and backed to the door– 'No, I need this, Masters. I ain't quite sure of the way the cards lay. You'll git it sometime but there'll be conditions.'

'Conditions? You're nuts! That there paper's my property!'

'Easy, Lacy,' Brent warned, as Frank made a move. 'I don't wanta drill either o' you gents but I'll do it if you make a play. Just back up agin that other wall, will you?'

A loaded Colt is a very forcible argument; Lee and Frank did as they were ordered but they retained sufficient independence to pick the two furthest apart walls they could so that the arc over which Brent's eyes would have to travel to watch both would be as wide as possible– 'I'm leaving now,' Brent told them; he fumbled the will into a pocket, shifted his gun from his right hand to his left while his right then felt for the doorknob behind him– 'I'll be back soon and tell you what you've got to do.'

'After your boss has told you what to do, huh?' Lee sneered.

A dull, angry flush crept up Brent's neck– 'I ain't got no boss,' he growled. 'I play things the way I want to! And I'm advising you to wait here till I come back; there'll be a feller with a rifle watching the winder and the door!'

'Same feller's holding a rifle at your back now?' Lee asked.

Brent had opened the door without looking behind him and for one fleeting instant he fell for the ancient ruse, his head started to turn but before his brain could countermand instinct, one of Lee's Colts seemed to leap to hand and its explosion was thunderous in the small room as the heavy bullet smashed the weapon out of Brent's hand.

Frank jumped across and snatched it up as Lee said– 'I'll have that will, Brent! And I'd admire to know why you wanted it!'

Brent tried to get away through the open door but Frank seized him ungently by the collar and hauled him back into the room– 'Give!' Lee ordered curtly, and slowly, reluctantly Brent handed over the paper. Lee opened it out and spelled the words to himself; they were simple enough, it left the Circle M to him absolutely, subject only to a lien Jeff had made to the First National Cattleman's Bank and Trust Company of Lansing. That was a bit of a shock, but as he folded the will and slid it back into an inside pocket Lee was still quite pleased with himself– 'Now talk, Brent,' he ordered, 'and talk fast. This business shouldn't be none of your business! How come you took cards?'

'That's my business,' Brent retorted. 'I ain't talking.'

'Then maybe you'll talk to the Law,' Lee replied. 'We'll go see Sheriff Barnes!'

Barnes looked helplessly bewildered as Lee explained why he had marched Brent into the Sheriff's Office with a gun in his back– 'Armed robbery?' he asked, 'but he ain't stole nothin'!'

'Naw, I got it back – but I'm bringing a charge all the same. Slap him in jail, Sheriff!'

'But I can't do that! He's...'

'A saloon keeper who's got ideas. You gonna do your duty and put him in jail?'

'Don't tell me what my duty is, young feller!' Barnes tried to bluster. 'I know what I should do and what I shouldn't, and I ain't gonna jail Brent just on account you say so!'

'He's got a witness,' Frank Lacy stated.

'I don't care if he's got a hundred witnesses,' Barnes answered. 'I don't reckon he's got any case to answer.'

'Ain't that for the Judge to say?' Lee demanded. 'Are you gonna jail Brent – or not?'

'Not!' Barnes stated flatly, or as near being defiant as was possible for him.

'C'mon, Frank,' Lee said bitterly. 'I allus heard there was towns where the law was crooked but up to now I never met one.'

'You better be careful what you say, Masters,' Barnes warned.

'Yeah? Why? Just so you don't have no trouble with your Boss? I'm leaving. And next time, Barnes, I'll leave my law to Judge Colt!'

As he and Frank Lacy tramped out, the derisive grin on Brent's face made his blood boil– 'I'm so damn mad I could tear him apart,' Lee gritted.

Frank took his arm– 'Easy, Lee,' he

cautioned. 'I met towns like this afore – even if you ain't. You gotta be careful how you buck the law and even more careful how you buck them as got pertection, and Brent sure has that.'

'Purdy! Judge Purdy! He's back of this,' Lee muttered. 'He's back of this I'll bet a man! Still, he kin wait. We'll go and see this First National Cattleman's Bank and Trust Company, and I'll be plumb surprised if it's more'n half the size of the title!'

Chapter 8

As Lee had suspected the Lansing Bank wasn't anything like so impressive as its name; it was housed in a small frame building quite a way down town, and the only solid part of it was the big, brick surrounded iron safe behind the single teller's grille– 'Banker Quinn's busy right now,' the teller told them. 'Guess he won't be long. Care to wait?'

Lee nodded; he and Frank sat down on the hard bench and had hardly time to roll and light cigarettes before the door of Quinn's office opened. The big, florid-faced banker was showing someone out, someone who, to judge by the obstinate set of his shoulders didn't want to go–

'Sorry I can't accommodate you, Mister Purdy,' Quinn said.

'But hell, man, why not?' Duke Purdy was as near to pleading as he could get.

'Sorry, nothing doing,' Quinn replied firmly.

Purdy swore, pushed his hat to the back of his head and swung round to face Lee, his face dark with anger– 'Following me around, huh?' he grated. 'Don't push it too hard, Masters, or you'll go the same way as your rustler brother – if you ain't started that already!'

Lee was on his feet in an instant– 'You'll take that back, Purdy,' he snapped, his hands poised over his Colt butts.

'Gentlemen! Easy, gentlemen!' Quinn spoke soothingly. 'Those were hard words you used, Purdy, but in the circumstances…'

Purdy, however, was too angry for soothing words– 'Circumstances be danged!' he blared. 'I'm being rustled blind and when I need a loan to help me hire more hands I git the brush-off. I s'pose Dad told you not to loan me money, huh? The old buzzard!'

'That'll be enough from you, Purdy,' Quinn told him, now as angry as himself. 'You better leave.'

'He's apologising to me for what he said,' Lee interposed. 'Apologising or drawing a gun!'

'I'll have no gunplay in here,' Quinn stated. 'What you do outside is your affair. Purdy, get out!'

Duke blustered a bit, but in the end he went– 'I'll see you afore sundown,' he told Lee viciously.

'Any time,' Lee replied. 'And you'll take back your words or drag an iron.'

'I ain't taking back the truth,' Purdy growled as he went out.

Quinn sighed– 'He's almost as awkward as

his father,' he said. 'You want to see me, gentlemen?'

'I'm Lee Masters and I'd like to talk to you about my brother's will.'

'Certainly. Come in. This fellow with you – Frank Lacy? Glad to know you.' Quinn looked at them keenly as soon as they were settled in chairs in his small, private office; Lee appraised him carefully; a lot of cow-town bankers were only as honest as they had to be, but Quinn looked straight enough.

'I got my brother's will here,' Lee went on. 'It leaves the ranch to me 'cept for a lien your Bank holds.'

'Yes, we hold a small lien over the Circle M, only a matter of a couple of hundred dollars; it's more than covered by what your brother had on his checking account. May I see the will?' He examined the document quickly, put it flat on his desk then stared at Lee across it– 'You're Jeff's brother all right,' he said, 'but you don't match up to the way Jeff talked to me about you.'

'No? How come?'

'Jeff said you were weak and easily led but from the way you handled Purdy I'd say that was wrong.'

Frank grinned– 'I'd say he was wrong too; you should have seen him being weak with old man Purdy's hired gunslick – Harrison!'

'Yes, I heard about that, and wondered,' Quinn commented. 'I guess the Judge thought Jeff had misled him about you. Now, about this will. It hasn't been proved yet so it isn't legal, but it's good enough for me. You can draw on Jeff's checking account if you want.'

'Yeah I do want, and thanks, Quinn. From the way the ranch is run down I'm surprised to hear Jeff had a checking account.'

'Seems he was pretty lucky gambling up to a little while before he died; he brought in plenty of cash.'

'How much is left?'

''Bout six hundred bucks – I think.'

'There's plenty of stores I need to buy, and from what I seen of it I'll be needing to restock the ranch some.'

'Maybe the bank'll help you there, we already have a lien – remember.'

'The Diamond's a better ranch!'

'Yes but... Oh I see – you mean Purdy? You couldn't help hearing I couldn't accommodate him. I have my reasons.'

'Seems like him and his Dad don't git along so good,' Frank suggested.

'Why should they? They've hated each other for years. Duke's mother owned that spread and when she died she willed it to Duke; old Judge very nearly hit the roof. He thought Duke should repudiate the will and let him have the ranch; Duke didn't see it that way, but he hasn't been much success as a rancher.'

Chapter 9

'Kinda queer him refusing to lend Purdy money,' Frank commented as they settled to a meal in the restaurant, 'that Diamond spread's worth plenty.'

'Yeah, there's lots of things I don't savvy in this town,' Lee answered. 'It could be Judge Purdy owns a piece of the bank.'

'Then why's Quinn so eager to lend you money? Way I figgered it, you and the Judge don't stack up to being bosom friends!'

'Could be the Judge just ain't got around to telling Quinn not to lend me money.'

'Could be. And what about the Judge's son? He'll be looking for you!'

Lee shrugged. 'I won't be hard to find,' he replied, 'and I hope he makes it soon, I don't want to wait in town till sundown then drive all that way to the Circle M in the dark.'

'I'll be sidin' you,' Frank said quietly.

'Thanks, feller, but I don't think Purdy's the kind to have one of his friends take a pot-shot at me from an alley.'

'Never kin tell. Way I figger him he's got a yellow streak, not a wide one, but a streak, otherwise he'd have made his play in the bank – banker or no; he was good and mad then and didn't pull his iron. He ducked out then, so he could do anythin' after he's brooded some.'

'Wonder if Laurel's in town?'

'That his wife? You knew her, didn't you?'

'Yah, and liked her a lot. I wouldn't want to...'

'Look, Lee, I'll take me a li'l mosey round and see what's cookin'. We stirred up quite considerable trouble for one morning. I won't be long.'

Lee watched Frank leave, then returned to his thoughts; he was still puzzling over Brent's incomprehensible action regarding the will, which document, incidentally, rested in Banker Quinn's safe prior to being sent to the County Seat to be proved. Brent had been surprised when the will had come to light and had acted quickly so perhaps he had exceeded any orders which might have been given to him; Lee could think of no reason why anyone else should want the Will unless to destroy it, thus giving the ranch back to Bella. He'd got thus far in his rather laborious train of thought when April walked into the restaurant–

'A fine morning's work you've done,' she said sharply, as she sat down in front of him.

'Me? How come?'

'Do you make a habit of quarrelling with neighbours?'

'When they say my brother was a rustler –
yeah I do!'

'But he was a rustler!'

'He what?' Lee stared at the girl in utter
amazement. 'Say that agin, girl!'

'Jeff was a rustler – if branding other
people's cows is rustling!'

'Hell! I don't believe it!' Somehow, however, Lee did believe it. Coming on top of the
statement in Jeff's letter, April's bold announcement was final. And yet – Jeff a
rustler? A cattle thief? Lee could hardly credit
it, but he could scarcely help but believe the
unpleasant reality– 'How'd you know?' he
asked.

'I was riding around one day and I came
on him in a little draw; he nearly shot me
before he saw who it was; there was a calf
and it had a different brand from its mother.'

Lee groaned, for that statement swept
away any last lingering doubt he could have
had– 'He have a small fire burnin'?' he
asked.

'Yes, and a piece of iron in his hand.'

'Did you see the brand on the cow?'

'It was a Flying W.'

'Ahuh. And what brand was he putting on
the calf?'

'I – I don't remember, but it – it was one I
didn't recognise; not a Circle M anyway.'

Lee rubbed his chin– 'Not a Circle M? I
don't git that unless...' Then he got

hurriedly to his feet as Laurel came hurrying into the restaurant–

'Lee!' she cried. 'Lee, you've got to back down from this stupid quarrel with Duke!'

'It weren't of my makin',' Lee told her sullenly; even in that short interval hostility had sparked between the two women–

'That's just what I've been telling him, Miz Purdy,' April said primly.

'And what's it got to do with you?' Laurel demanded.

'You two ladies oughta git acquainted,' Lee said awkwardly.

'We've already met – in Thomas's Store,' April replied. 'Mrs Purdy has seen fit to buy the gingham Mrs Thomas had put aside for my new dress!'

'So sorry about that but it was just what I wanted for kitchen curtain!' Laurel told her. 'Now, Lee, I can't have all this gunplay happening. Whyn't you leave town?'

'Why don't you leave men to take care of their own business?' April interrupted.

'It is my business! One of them's my husband!'

'And one of them nearly was. So if one of them gets killed you still have one left.'

Laurel swung at the girl, a swing which if it had landed would have knocked the smaller and lighter April for a loop; but it didn't land; April blocked it as neatly as a boxer then followed it by ducking her head

100

and butting Laurel just where her stays pinched most tightly. In a moment they were fighting like a couple of cats, with Lee doing a not very effective best to separate them, an effort during which he collected a scratch that ran from eyebrow to chin, half a dozen kick bruises on his legs and a badly bitten wrist. Only when they had at last been separated did he become aware that he'd some help in stopping the noisy fight which had done considerable damage to the restaurant furniture and caused a large and amused crowd to collect outside the restaurant window, a crowd which made no secret of its coarse enjoyment of the revelations inevitable in the course of such a contest; some of the remarks were so much to the point that both girls blushed furiously and together they sought the privacy of the back room to repair the damage they had done to each other. Lee mopped at the blood which trickled down his neck then faced the man who had helped him to stop the fight – it was Duke Purdy! Before either could say anything, the restaurant keeper claimed attention– 'Who's gonna pay for this?' he demanded, indicating smashed crockery, a drunken table and several collapsed chairs.

Duke glared at him– 'It ain't nothin' to do with me,' he stated angrily.

'Your wife done some of the smashin'!' the restaurant owner retorted.

'She didn't start the fight!' Duke snapped.

'There ain't no tellin' who started it,' Lee said quietly. 'How much, Joe? I'll pay!'

'The hell you'll pay!' Purdy blared. 'Think I'm a pauper? I always pay my debts!'

'Aw for Pete's sake!' Joe groaned. 'Gimme ten bucks and we'll call it quits.'

'Better share this then,' Lee suggested, pulling out a ten-spot.

'Awright,' Purdy growled, and matched the bill. 'I ain't forgot what happened in the Bank.'

'Nor me,' Lee replied curtly, but he looked at Purdy in some doubt. Now – now that he had learned that Purdy's accusation had some basis of fact he found that he didn't particularly want to shoot the fellow; and, moreover, in some peculiar way he knew that Purdy was sorry for what he had said and wished it unsaid even though he firmly believed he had spoken the truth. Purdy, Lee thought, wasn't a coward, but he was pretty sure he wasn't as fast and accurate with a gun as Lee was, and when two men face each other in an empty street, speed and accuracy mean life or death– 'I – I'm findin' out the Circle M don't have too savoury a reputation,' Lee said quietly, as Joe started to clear up the mess. He saw surprise gleam in Purdy's eyes, surprise and some relief.

'I was good and mad with Quinn,' Purdy said irrelevantly; but even so, Lee could guess how much even such a distant approach to an apology had cost him.

'Yeah, bankers kin git you that way. I aim to throw a straight loop, Purdy; there ain't gonna be no runnin' irons used on the Circle M no more.'

Purdy's eyes met Lee's squarely and, for the first time, Lee realised that they were honest, attractive eyes. Purdy was big, noisy, and belligerent, a bit of a blusterer, but that, after the way his father had treated him, was perhaps understandable. But Purdy was straight, and as April and Laurel came back out of Joe's kitchen they were astonished to see the two causes of their own quarrel gripping hands in the most friendly way which, in some unaccountable fashion, annoyed both girls exceedingly, it made the damage to their dignity and dresses even less worth while. However, they both realised that more than torn clothes had been at stake; Laurel dredged up a watery smile that soon became genuine when Purdy took her arm and said—'Guess I was wrong about Lee, honey; he ain't such a bad feller.'

Lee smiled mournfully— 'Better take it easy, Duke, we don't want it told around that we let our women do our fightin' for us!'

'And what gives you the right to think I'm your woman?' April demanded, flaring up instantly.

'Wa'al, I didn't mean that,' Lee mumbled.

'Then what did you mean?'

'He meant you took his part,' Laurel told her soothingly. 'He couldn't fight me himself, and I don't want him to fight my husband.' She looked up at Duke as she said this, and the glow of her eyes effectively disposed of any lingering hope Lee might have had that her marriage to Duke would fail; somehow he felt surprisingly cheerful about the knowledge.

Frank Lacy came back then, accepted the situation with a gulp and a blink of astonishment as he sidled up to Lee– 'We better pull outa town, Lee,' he whispered. 'I don't know quite what's happenin' but there's somethin' being cooked up.'

Lee eased out of the group– 'How come?' he asked quietly.

Frank scratched his head– 'I dunno – quite,' he admitted, 'but everyone in town seems to think Judge Purdy's layin' for you. Hell! here's the Sheriff now!'

Barnes came into the restaurant, slowly and with quite obvious reluctance– 'I want you, Masters,' he said, but his voice held no more conviction than his tired eyes or drooping moustache.

'Nice to know I'm popular,' Lee countered. 'And why?'

'For murderin' Ed Cowin!'

'Cowin? You nuts? I found him dead!'

'So you said.'

'It's the truth! And anyway why should I want to murder Cowin?'

'So's he couldn't say you ain't Lee Masters.'

'Barnes, have you gone stark ravin' mad?' Lee demanded. 'Cowin didn't know me anyway; he wouldn't have known me from Tom Scuttlebut!'

'I figger you're an imposter just tryin' to grab Jeff Masters' ranch!' Barnes voice rose, the almost squeaky voice of a weak man forcing himself to run a bluff which he knows is a bad one.

'That he isn't,' Laurel Purdy cut in. 'I've known Lee three years.'

'Yeah, and I've known him since afore Jeff died,' Duke Purdy said. 'Someone's feeding you crowbait, Barnes! I reckon it wouldn't be a bad idea if you produced some evidence afore you start slingin' murder charges around!'

'Beat it, Sheriff,' Lee advised, 'afore I feed you to Joe's cat!'

'No!' Frank Lacy spoke explosively, 'Don' let him git away yet, Lee! Easy, Sheriff, just elevate your hands and lemme take your hardware!' A Colt in one hand, Lacy deftly took the Sheriff's gun and eased the scared Law Officer over until he had backed him to the wall beside the door where he could not be seen from outside. The crowd had gone, but the street was still fairly busy–

'You crazy, Frank?' Lee asked, puzzled, and almost annoyed by the way his henchman had taken control.

'No I ain't,' Frank retorted, 'but you would be if you let Barnes go.'

'What'n blazes do you mean?'

'You reckon Barnes thought this up his own self? Course he didn't! Some'un said to him– "Barnes, you grab your hat and a nice shiny star and go and arrest Lee Masters. Never mind what for – just git him into jail." Ain't that right, Barnes?' He swung round on the scared Sheriff who was heard to mutter–

'That was purty near right.'

'See?' Frank queried fiercely. 'As long as we got the Sheriff we're awright. Whoever put him up to this – Judge Purdy I'd guess – won't know it didn't take, but as soon as Barnes walks outa here alone it'll be clear he's missed out.'

'Maybe you got somethin' there, Frank,' Lee said slowly, then the restaurant keeper took a hand–

'I ain't a patient man, gents,' he announced, 'and I'm gettin' mighty tired of all this argyfyin' in my place. There's a back way out and you're welcome to use it.'

Lee swung to Purdy– 'Duke,' he said, 'I need some help. Will you...?'

Purdy, once he had decided to like them

anyhow liked them all the way– 'Shore, Lee,' he said quietly.

'The Circle M buckboard's in Hughes' livery stable; I need supplies; here's a hundred bucks, would you git the buckboard, buy me flour, bacon, coffee, beans... Hell, Duke, you know what's needed on a ranch where there ain't no food. Me and Frank'll be just outa town on the Circle M trail.'

Duke took the money– 'Sure, Lee,' he repeated, and ambled out.

'What about me?' April asked.

'You ain't in on this,' Lee told her. 'Watch for the buckboard; when it's loaded hop aboard and come on outa town.'

'I'll look after her, Lee,' Laurel told him with a smile. 'I'll be glad to.'

'Fine,' Lee said. 'C'mon, Frank, and you, Barnes. Back way for us. And, Barnes,' he added warningly, 'I wouldn't want you should make any noise!'

Chapter 10

'We're leavin' too,' Duke Purdy said, as Lee raised an eyebrow at seeing two buckboards outside the town, where he had expected to see only one. Duke was driving the Circle M vehicle, Laurel the Diamond's. April sat beside her and they chattered away together as if they had been friends all their lives, instead of having tried to scratch each other's eyes out only hours before– 'Reckon me and Lansing ain't gonna agree for a bit,' Duke added as he clapped on the brake and pulled the mustangs to a stop. 'I seen Harrison looking at me kinda interested, sure must have been a pasting you handed him, Lee, he's still marked up!'

'Next time I'll use a gun,' Lee replied, watching sourly as Frank helped April down from the Diamond's buckboard. 'Awright, Barnes, you kin git now!'

Apparently the cowed Law Officer reckoned he'd better make some attempt to uphold his dignity– 'You'll be sorry you treated the Law thisaway, young feller,' he stated, as blusteringly as he knew how.

'Yeah?' Lee jeered. 'Same's you were after you wouldn't charge Brent, huh?'

Barnes's face showed a dull flush as he turned and trudged back towards town without another word– 'You take the buckboard, Frank,' Lee said, 'I want to talk with Duke.' Together, he and Frank helped April up into the Circle M vehicle then Lee climbed up behind Duke and Laurel– 'You been losing many cows, Duke?' he asked, when the dust cloud caused by the abrupt start of the other buckboard had subsided.

'Yeah,' Duke said curtly as he let the horses out. 'Too many. I had me a round-up afore I went down to Tracy but I didn't figger it out close till I came back; it's bad; I musta had close to a thousand cows stolen.'

Lee whistled– 'That's quite some cows,' he muttered. 'But how?'

'Danged if I know,' Duke admitted. 'They ain't been drove past Lansing, that I'll swear.'

'Other way? Black Rock Mountains.'

'It ain't possible,' Duke stated flatly, 'unless they got some flying machine to carry 'em over.'

'Then where... Hell, man! If there's been brand-blottin' it ain't possible to hide that many cows – not in a herd my size. I ain't got that many cows anyway!'

'I know you ain't. I figgered your brother only run three or four hundred so if he was on the rustle – and I'm saying straight out I think he was – he musta drove 'em some place.'

Lee winced– 'That's the way I figger it too,' he muttered. 'Way I figger it, Duke, Jeff was on the rustle for a spell and then he quit, which was why he was murdered by them that was in cahoots with him.'

'Murdered?' Duke queried sharply.

'Yeah. Jeff was murdered awright. What's more he expected he would be.' Lee told Purdy about his discovery of the thorn in Jeff's saddle.

Purdy whistled– 'What a hell of a way to die,' he muttered, 'and after he'd probably been expectin' to be dry-gulched. Wa'al, here's where we part, Lee. I guess you know how I feel now, and you know I'm ready to help when you want me!'

Lee gripped the offered hand briefly as the Diamond buckboard stopped– 'I know that, Duke,' he said, as he got down, 'and I'm grateful, but all the same this here is my problem and I'm aimin' to swing it myself. If I can't, I'll come for help. So long, Duke, and so long, Laurel! You keep close to home!'

Laurel flashed a smile at him– 'Same to you, Lee,' she said, 'and if that Miss April was there I guess you wouldn't mind so much at that.'

The Circle M buckboard had pulled up close behind, so close that April must have heard the words for her face was flushed as Lee climbed up and took the reins from Lacy.

'She needn't have said that about me,' April stated sharply. 'Your ranch isn't my home, Mister Masters, and I'll be leaving soon!'

Lee tried his best to assume an expression of indifference he was far from feeling– 'Suit yourself, Miss,' he said, just failing to keep his voice level. He slapped the reins, gave the buckskins their heads and concentrated hard on his driving – or tried to; in fact, with April's slim body pressed against his on the narrow seat and thrown against him whenever the buckboard lurched which, on that rough road, was frequently, he found it very hard to think about anything else but her and how much he would miss her if she left the Circle M. Even had he been paying full attention to the trail it is doubtful whether he would have caught the glint of sunlight on the rifle barrel which projected from a clump of greasewood a quarter of a mile up from the trail. As it was, the first he knew about it was the sharp clang of a rifle and the sudden collapse of one of the buckskins. Then things happened in a splinter of time; the buckboard, brought up all standing, pitched its occupants violently forward; Lee found the ground come up and hit him smack on the face, yet even as he'd flown through the air some instinct had swept one of his arms protectively round April and thus enabled him to break the force of her fall. Nearly unconscious, he had sufficient sense left to heave her slender body out of the reach of the second buckskin which, terrified and frantic, was lunging and kicking in a fury to escape from the harness which bound him to his dead companion and the buckboard which, riding up on the body of the dead horse, had overset and now lay on its side wheels spinning.

Lee spat out a mouthful of dust and rubbed his eyes clear; he had fallen comparatively softly but moved his limbs experimentally and found they all worked, as the rifle clanged again he heard the bullet smack into the buckboard floor and as his brain cleared he realised that he and April were completely exposed to the rifleman. The girl was unconscious, knocked clean out but a quick examination assured him that she hadn't broken any bones. He got to his knees, gathered her in his arms and managed to shuffle round behind the buckboard where the pile of goods, tossed out of the vehicle, provided cover of a sort. Lacy had been pitched out on that side and lay sprawled out, unconscious; Lee put April down and settled her as comfortably as he could before he dragged Frank back under cover. As he did so, Lacy's eyes blinked open– 'Who threw the range at me?' he demanded weakly.

'Dunno,' Lee replied shortly, 'but I aim to find out.' A slow rage had begun to fill his brain, a rage that grew and grew, demanding outlet in action, violent, vengeful action.

'How's April?' Lacy asked, trying to get up.

'She ain't hurt bad; just knocked cold.' Lee drew the one Colt that had stayed in its holster, broke it, extracted the cartridges, wiped them clean on his neck-cloth, freed the action of dust, span the cylinder and reloaded– 'I'm gonna git me that pot-shootin' buzzard,' he announced grimly.

'Be right with you, boss!'

'You won't! You ain't in no shape. I want you should stay here and look after April.'

'I don't need no one to look after me!' the girl said surprisingly. 'I'm all right now.' She was, however, pale as a sheet, but tried gamely to sit up.'

'Don't!' Lee warned. 'Them boxes ain't high. Frank, while I'm on my way, pile the stuff so's to make better cover, will you? And cut that horse loose!' With that he crawled away, keeping the buckboard between him and the rifleman until he had covered the stretch of open range which separated him from the nearest patch of mesquite. He reached it after what seemed an age, an age of acute discomfort; he was sweating at every pore, sweat had clotted the dust on his face, soaked his clothes, every muscle ached and the crawling had bruised his knees. He parted the tough mesquite stems, rolled over on his belly and looked back; the trail ran along the bottom of a shallow valley and he looked down upon the upset buckboard; having freed the remaining buckskin which had not gone far before it started to graze, Lacy was slowly and cautiously shifting the boxes and bags of supplies so as to form a better shelter. Beyond the buckboard the range rose smoothly to the greasewood clump which covered the rifleman; behind the greasewood the ground continued to rise. It was clothed in scrub which thickened into undergrowth towards the tree-studded crest. While he got his breath back Lee planned the circuit he would have to make to bring him round behind the rifleman, and cursed again his own lack of a long gun; with a Winchester he could have probed that greasewood from end to end. But he hadn't got a Winchester so he pulled himself back through the mesquite and set out on his walk which he reckoned would be all of a mile long for he would have to back-trail quite a piece before he could cross to the other side of the valley without being seen. His rage had settled to an icy determination to get the man who had fired on him, but as he walked his brain was speculating on the curious feature of the attack; the rifleman was clearly a first-class shot. The first bullet which had downed the buckskin, had been aimed to a hair's breadth; it had drilled the horse cleanly through the brain; yet the second, and so far only other shot, might just as well have been fired into the air. If the rifleman had intended to kill him, Lee knew, he could have done it with the utmost ease during the seconds he had lain helpless, in clear view, after being thrown from the buckboard. So it appeared that murder was not the object of the hold-up. What then was the object? Back in town Judge Purdy had made a clumsy and ineffective try at throwing him in jail; he would have had enough time – but only just enough – to send a rifleman on a fast horse, ahead of the buckboard with orders to hold it up, but with what object?

Just before he reached the spot where he planned to cross the valley, Lee heard another rifle shot; he stopped, looked back from behind a juniper bush and saw the rifleman emerge from his cover; the fellow held his weapon ready for a further shot; he had his neckcloth drawn up over his nose and was looking in Lee's direction; as Lee watched, the man raised his rifle and fired three more shots with about ten seconds between them. From behind Lee, on the back trail to Lansing, came the flat report of three answering shots– 'Colt,' Lee muttered. 'Looks like I guessed right; first feller's just holdin' us up for the others. Posse? Could be, though I doubt Barnes had time to git back to town and raise one so quick.'

As he tried to work out the situation, Lee started back towards April and Lacy; the time to hunt down the rifleman was past for he reckoned much worse trouble was due nearer at hand. He was still a quarter of a mile from the buckboard and, luckily for him, still under cover when two horsemen appeared from the direction of Lansing; they were flogging their tired mounts which they had clearly pushed hard all the way from town; one of them Lee recognised at once as Purdy's gunman, Harrison, and the other man was the one Lacy had dealt with at the 'Lulu'. They reined in their horses some fifty or sixty yards away from the pile of goods behind which April and Lacy were sheltering, and as he snaked forward from clump to clump of greasewood Lee heard Harrison bawl– 'C'mon out, Masters! C'mon out! We want you!'

Lacy's head appeared for a moment above a flour sack, but he bobbed down again when he saw that the two horsemen were out of Colt range–

'It's Masters we want,' Harrison shouted. 'You and the gal kin git up and git! C'mon out, Masters! You ain't got a chance!'

A flick of his wrist sent the second horseman moving off to one side from which the makeshift shelter would have been wide open to his rifle. Lee swore as a patch of tangled mesquite made his progress even slower. Harrison was impatient – unless Lee got within Colt range quickly– 'Masters!' Harrison yelled. 'I'm gonna give you two minutes to come out! Then we start shootin' and it'll be too bad about the gal!'

Lee took a chance that the attention of both horsemen would be on the buckboard; he rose to his feet and at a crouching run made the cover of a manzanita bush only a hundred yards behind Harrison, only a hundred yards but it was still double the effective range of a Colt and there was no further cover between him and the gunman–

'One minute gone, Masters!' Harrison shouted, and drew the rifle from its scabbard behind his saddle.

Lee bit off an oath, moved out from behind his bush and walked forward; he knew that if he ran he couldn't hope to shoot straight, yet it was one of the hardest things he ever did to walk steadily on when at any moment Harrison might turn, see him, and shoot him like a clay pigeon. Ten yards, twenty yards, thirty yards he covered, his heart thumping like a trip hammer. Forty yards and he drew his Colt, raised it shoulder high ready to chop down as soon as the range was short enough. Fifty yards and the rifleman across the valley saw him. The man's hurried shot only just missed for Lee felt the wind of the bullet.

'Masters!' Harrison called sharply, not

quite understanding why the shot had been fired.

'Right here, Harrison!' Lee snapped, and as Harrison turned in his saddle bringing his rifle round, Lee's Colt swung down, belched flame and smoke; it was still long range for a short gun but Harrison and his horse made a pretty big target. Lee's first bullet must have burned the horse for it lunged violently enough to throw Harrison's rifle off aim. Lee fired twice again before Harrison could jerk out his spent cartridge and pump another one into the breech of his Winchester, and the second shot smashed his right shoulder and very nearly knocked him out of the saddle. Lee sensed, rather than saw, that Lacy had got to one knee and was firing his Colt at the second horseman. Harrison, his right arm useless, dragged out a Colt with his left hand but before he could raise it Lee's fourth shot took him full in the chest. For a moment he stayed upright in the saddle, then his muscles relaxed and he slumped and slipped to the ground. The second horseman still had the game in his hands had he had the nerve to play it; he was mounted, he had a rifle, he could easily have done for two men who were afoot and had only short guns, but he hadn't the nerve; maybe it was the sight of Harrison's body crumpled on the ground, maybe it was the bullets Lacy fired at him as fast as he could pull trigger. Whatever it was he jammed his spurs home and forced his tired horse into a lumbering gallop. Lee watched him go, only for an instant then he ran for the Winchester Harrison had dropped and, using Harrison's body for cover, he fired the rest of the magazine back up at the rifleman who had started the trouble. In the silence after the last shot, he heard the rapid drum of departing hoofbeats. He got to his feet, stripped Harrison's cartridge belt from the gunman's body and recharged the Winchester magazine as he walked towards where Lacy stood reloading his Colt– 'Wa'al, what d'you know?' Lacy tried to keep his voice steady, but it quavered a bit and Lee noticed that his fingers, trying to push cartridges into the Colt, were trembling.

'Dunno – quite,' Lee answered. 'You awright, April?'

'Yes, I'm – I'm fine. D-does this sort of thing often happen around here?'

'Me, I'm a stranger,' Lee reminded her. 'And it was me they wanted!'

'That feller – the first one – he could have killed us easy,' Lacy said.

'Sure he could, but that wasn't what he meant to do. Seems like they want me alive!'

'But why?'

'Heaven knows. C'mon, let's git the buckboard back on its wheels and load the stuff back on. This place ain't healthy!'

Chapter 11

'So you found the will, huh?' Bella Masters asked quietly.

'Yeah,' Lee replied, 'I found the will.'

'And does it leave the ranch to you?'

'It does.'

Bella looked down at the floor, her fingers busy folding and unfolding a handkerchief– 'Then I ain't got no home?' She was sober, quietly dressed with hardly any make-up on her face and, to Lee, surprisingly friendly, so friendly he didn't quite know what to do about it; if she had been drunk and aggressive he felt he would have been able to deal with her much more easily– 'Wa'al, it ain't 'xactly that, ma'am,' he said.

'What is it then? And surely you could call me "Bella", Lee? After all we are related. I – I s'pose I wasn't what you'd call a good wife to Jeff but I was fond of him even – even if he didn't treat me quite right. I – I ain't got no place to go Lee, and I wouldn't want to go back to the old life Jeff saved me from. Dance hall gals don't git much fun outa life you know, you always gotta look like you're happy when mostly all you wanta do is haul off'n sock the fellers that try to maul you

120

around. Just 'cause I was a dance hall gal don't mean I was bad, Lee.'

And looking at her Lee almost believed her– 'Why sure you kin stay,' he told her. 'Stay as long as you like.'

'I'll work, Lee, I'll work hard; I ain't afraid of work. I kin cook – some, and sew and such like. But I'm keepin' you – you got work to do. Me and April will set about cleaning up this place a bit. Jeff always said he preferred it untidy.'

Thankfully, Lee escaped from the chaos of the ranch-house–

'You oughta thrown her out neck and crop,' Frank Lacy growled as they rode away.

'And April?' Lee queried.

Frank flushed but said nothing for a mile or more until they reached the throat of the canyon at the head of the valley– 'What are we looking for?' he asked, as Lee pulled Black Powder to a stop and gazed around him.

'Somethin' Jeff wrote me about in a letter he left, somethin' to do with a place called Owl Canyon we used to play in when we was kids.'

'How come?'

'I got a feelin' that if we find it we got a lead on what all the queer goin's on on this range are about. Frank, I could easy understand Purdy, Judge Purdy, wanting me dead, but I'm danged if I kin see why he should want me alive. C'mon, let's ride.'

121

The entrance to the canyon was so narrow that at the throat the trail, squeezed by the tumbling waters of the creek, was only just wide enough for a couple of horses; to their left the hillside rose almost sheer, so steep that only a few stunted shrubs could cling to the crevices in the black rock. Over beyond the creek the other wall rose nearly as steeply, but after a half a mile the hills opened out a little and they found themselves in a narrow valley. The creek still skirted the right hand wall but between it and the other, less steep and tree clad side, there was a meadow of lush grass. Lee pushed his hat back and scratched his head– 'Queer there ain't no cows on this good feed,' he said. 'I guess it is a bit like Owl Canyon. Now what'n hell was Jeff gettin' at?' Recollection was beginning to stir faintly at the back of his mind, some vague memory was struggling upwards through the morass of more recent memories that overlaid it – 'Yeah,' he said, speaking more to himself than to Frank, 'Yeah, Jeff had him an old shot-gun Pa'd thrown away; Pa didn't reckon we was old enough to have guns. It was an old muzzle loader and it kicked like a mule, we hid it with the powder and shot up in Owl Canyon. There was a lot of quail there and we used to git us a few and cook 'em over a camp fire, playin' we was prospectors lookin' for the Lingerin' Lode. And yeah I got it now, Frank, there was a fault runnin' offen Owl Canyon, we found it accidentally, we never would have found it if we'd been lookin' for it. Yeah, I know what Jeff meant now, and I'm beginnin' to guess what them jaspers want.'

He rode on slowly, his eyes busily searching the left-hand wall of the canyon; this was too steep to be climbed but not so steep that the rock hadn't become clothed with a thick mat of trees which spread from the base of the wall out upon the meadow so that it was hard to see exactly where the hillside met the floor of the valley. But for all his keen examination Lee couldn't see any point that bore resemblance to the place his memory recalled– 'There was a big juniper near it,' he told Frank. 'But I don't see no juniper here, only hornbeam and quakin' ash; there's some live oaks along a piece, and a few dwarf cedars but I don't see… Hell! But I do! Look, Frank! There is a juniper – and the hell of a big one too!' He swung out of his saddle by the bush, almost big enough to be called a tree; behind it the scrub was as dense as anywhere else; looking up he could see no break in the valley wall, yet– 'I'll just nacherley bet my socks this is the place,' he said. 'It's just gotta be.'

'It don't look no different to me,' Frank said as he, in turn, dismounted. 'Hell, it does though! Don't move, Lee!'

Lee froze as Frank's Colt roared, and looking round he saw a rattlesnake writhing in its death agonies, only feet from his body– 'It didn't even rattle,' Lee said shakily.

'Sometimes they don't,' Frank told him, punching out his exploded cartridge– 'You dang near trod on that one and he riz up pronto. But his bein' here means there's gotta be clear rock somewheres close by, snakes don't go for wooded country, they like to sun themselves.'

'Thanks, feller,' Lee said. 'I ain't hankerin' none to be shot but I reckon I'd rather be shot than bit by a snake. Keep that gun handy while I search around, he may have friends. And look! There's been cows here!'

'Could be they wanted to eat some leaves. Cows go for juniper leaves.'

'Then whyn't they pick 'em from the front side; there's a trail here, Frank, and it's been covered mighty careful. Looka here where there's bare earth under the trees, it's been swept with a branch – you kin see the twig marks. And here – look on this thorn bush, there's hair from a horse's tail – palomino I'd say.'

'Looks like we're on to somethin', Lee.'

'We sure as hell are, and if we ain't careful, Frank, we'll have some'un on to us. Git our broncs under cover will you? Grass out on the meadow's purty thick and oughta hide their tracks, but you see you don't leave no sign comin' in among the trees.'

While Frank went to get the horses out of sight of anyone who might have followed them into the canyon, Lee searched forward along the cattle trail he had found; in less than fifty yards he found he was in near darkness and looking up he saw knife edge steep walls of rock on either side of him. He was in a natural rock fault, just like a knife cut, heading slantingly into the hillside, its open edge so narrow and so masked by the trees as to be invisible; once fairly within the entrance all attempt to mark the cattle trail had been abandoned and Lee saw that a considerable number of cattle had passed over it though the sign told him that none had been along it for some weeks– 'Kinda spooky ain't it?' Frank asked as he came up with the horses.

Lee's face was grim as he took his mount and swung up into the saddle– 'Know what it is?' he asked. 'Just a nice secret back door to the Lansing range.'

'You mean this is the way your brother...'

'Drove rustled stock? Yeah. Just that, Frank. No wonder Purdy couldn't trace how his steers was being rustled. They could have been rustled offen his range and driven here in one night.'

'Yeah, but where we goin'?'

'We're gonna find out where this fault leads, and it's my guess we'll find it leads out on to the range on the other side of Black Rock Mountains!'

From then on they rode in silence, each busy with his thoughts; for Lee they were not pleasant thoughts. From what he knew and from what had happened since he had hit the Lansing range he could only deduce that Jeff, and Jeff alone, had known about the fault. Probably, almost certainly, other members of the rustling organisation had done the actual stealing, had driven the stock to the Circle M from whence Jeff pushed them on through the fault on his own. That was the secret the others wanted to get from him, that was the secret for which he was killed, and which 'they' – whoever 'they' were – believed he had passed on to Lee. Now that he had started on the trail Lee meant to follow it to the end, he meant to find out the whole sordid story, to drain to the bitter dregs the draught of knowledge that his brother had been a cattle thief–

'If I'm gonna live on this range and run the Circle M,' he told himself, 'I gotta square up for Jeff – poor fool. He musta been plumb crazy. Still and all, at least he give it up 'fore he died.'

The fault ran very nearly straight for close on two miles, rising all the time and then, almost as abruptly as it began, it came to an end and they found they had ridden into another valley. This was close to a mile long, less than half a mile wide, floored with rich bunch grass and with steep, tree-clad walls; a few cattle grazed at the far end where feathery willows showed the presence of water. Nearby, smoke rose from a small cabin beside which there was a pole corral containing four or five saddle horses– 'Here's where we maybe ain't gonna be so welcome,' Lee said quietly, and checked his guns. Frank did the same, whistling softly as he did so–

'Kind of a queer set-up, ain't it?' he asked.

'Looks simple enough to me. Stock was rustled offen the Lansing range, pushed through inta this valley where it's my guess they blotted the brands before drivin' 'em on down the far side of the mountains.'

'Yeah, that's clear but...'

'But what?'

Frank shifted uncomfortably in his saddle– 'Wa'al, seems like your brother was the only one who knew about that fault we just come through; these fellers here, they musta known where the cows come from?'

'True enough – but what then?'

'Wa'al, Jeff's been dead for weeks. Why ain't they been to see why he ain't drove no more stock through?'

'I see what you mean, but I dunno the answer.'

When they were a quarter of a mile from the cabin a short, thick-set man came to the open door, stared at them then, apparently satisfied, waved and turned back inside the cabin– 'I ain't fallin' for that,' Lee said quietly. 'Circle left a piece, Frank, there could be a rifle looking at us from behind that door.'

They swung their horses and approached the back of the cabin where there was a blank wall, dismounting fifty yards from it and walking on, watching alertly for any sign of danger. Nothing happened before they reached the hard packed earth which surrounded the small building; inside, a frying pan clanged on a stove, followed by the hiss of steaks being tossed into hot fat, then they heard a grumbling voice demand–

'Where's the hell they done went?' Heavy feet thumped across the board floor– 'Hey, Jeff!' the voice called, 'Where at you gotten to? Chuck's about ready!'

Lee waved Frank back, walked quickly round to the front of the cabin, stopping as he turned the last corner and found himself facing the thick-set man– 'Hell! You ain't Jeff!' the man swore, his hand dropping like a stone to the gun that hung low on his right hip.

Lee drew and fired on the instant but he was only just fast enough for the other had got his gun out and up before Lee's bullet took him; he was falling as he pulled the trigger and his bullet only dug dirt at Lee's feet. As the man fell, Lee jumped for the cabin door, his Colt ready, but the dark, musty-smelling interior of the cabin did not conceal any other enemy– 'He went for a gun,' Lee explained as Frank came round to look at the body. 'He was dang fast too, I hadn't time to try shootin' the gun outa his hand.'

'Huh. That one won't talk,' Frank answered. 'But that steak reminds me it's a long time since breakfast; seein' he put it on for us it'd be a shame not to eat it.'

Lee was inside, searching the frowsy contents of the cabin; there wasn't much to search, a bunk-bed, a rough table and a couple of chairs, a Fearnaught stove, some rough shelves tacked to the wall by the single window, and a saddle dumped in one corner– 'He lived alone,' Lee commented, 'and purty rough too, and drank some at that,' he pointed to a litter of empty whisky bottles in one corner.

'Here's somethin',' Frank said, rootling among a pile of dusty sacks in another corner from which he produced a branding iron– 'Stampin' iron,' he said, 'and I guess it's the answer to one problem. Lookit, Lee, a Circle M inside a Diamond, and if the feller usin' it was clever he could cover up a Flyin' W as well!'

'There ain't no iron could couple them brands, you cluck!' Lee told him impatiently.

129

'Just you look, Lee. See here, the Diamond's outside and our Circle M brand inside; I hadn't noticed before that the Diamond was so much bigger'n our Circle.'

Lee examined the stamping iron Frank handed him; it was a big, heavy instrument, clumsy too– 'Be a good hand if he could overlap the brands without blottin' 'em,' he commented.

'Yeh, but it could be done; this iron's been used a lot – and recent too. Let's go have us a look at them cows!'

When they had rounded up half a dozen cows Frank roped and threw them in turn while Lee had a look at the brands; when he'd straightened up from beside the last prime three-year-old, his face was grim, his eyes cold– 'Yeah,' he told Frank as he signed to him to release the animal– 'Yeah, that's it awright. Feller as used that iron was an artist, you gotta look plumb close to see the old brands underneath. This musta been quite a steal.' He gripped his saddle horn, swung up and turned Black Powder towards the cabin. 'Five of them cows had been Diamond's, the other a Flyin' W.'

Frank said– 'Funny they ain't been moved on.'

'Brands are purty fresh. My guess is this feller worked alone – same's Jeff did. Workin' alone he'd be able to brand only a few each day and from what we kin see of the way he lived he didn't like work much. Reminds me, I ain't searched his body yet.'

A search of the dead brand-blotter's body revealed that his name had been Clausen, that Lee got from a bill-head from a store in a place called Snake Butte; Clausen had quite a lot of money in a worn billfold; Lee took it without compunction for it would go some way towards paying Duke Purdy back for the stock he had lost. He was just replacing the bill-fold in Clausen's pocket when a piece of paper fell out of a flap at the back of it; Lee spread it and read the crabbed writing– 'Clausen, tell your boss I can't take no more for a month or two. I think Delmer's smelt a rat.' It was signed only with the initial 'T', and dated about six weeks before–

'There's why Clausen wasn't worried 'cause Jeff didn't show up,' Lee said. 'He musta told him what the note said.'

'And this "T" feller is the one been buyin' the rustled stock?'

'Looks like it – though who Delmer is and why he smells a rat, I dunno, Frank. We'll ramble down to this Snake Butte place and see how the cards fall.'

'Suits me, but it's away past noon awready and my stomach is plumb certain my throat's cut.'

'Awright, let's eat, then we'll bury Clausen, sleep the night and go on fresh.'

After they had eaten, they buried Clausen

131

then cleared up the cabin – which was a job long overdue; the hidden valley was quite high up in the mountains and it grew cold when the sun went down so that they were glad of the stove and the one full bottle of whisky they found–

'You reckon we're near to cleanin' up this rustlin'?' Frank queried as they ate their evening meal.

'I reckon we've cleared up this end – or near enough. We got a good idea who's buyin' the stuff; but we ain't cleared up the other end; Jeff was in it awright, but we dunno who else.'

'Maybe his widow knows?'

'She probably does but I dunno how to make her tell; I'd guess Brent was in it – and Wilkinson too, but I got a feeling they ain't the only ones.'

'What you mean, Lee?'

'Brent's a saloon-keeper, and Wilkinson ain't much. Some'un with brains was runnin' this and I don't reckon it was Jeff. Jeff wasn't long on brains or he wouldn't have got himself snagged with that Bella.'

'She ain't much like her sister, is she?'

Lee glanced keenly at Frank whose face had flushed– 'You like April a lot don't you, Frank?'

'Yeah I do, but I ain't kiddin' myself she likes me much. Why should she when she kin git the boss?'

'Me? Hell no! She don't go for me.'

Frank sighed– 'Wish I could be sure of that, Lee. But anyway, what's the use, I ain't nothin' but a forty-a-month puncher and she – why she's eddicated, teaches school and all. Me, I never did above Second Grade.'

'Love's a funny thing, feller. Back in Tracy I figgered I was in love with Laurel – her that married Duke Purdy; I still like her a lot but I ain't in love with her.'

'You in love with April, Lee?' Frank's voice was trembly, as if he didn't want to ask the question but had to.

Lee shrugged– 'That ain't a question I kin answer,' he said. 'Are you?'

'Yeah I am,' Frank told him bluntly. 'Soon's I seen her trying to catch up that mare I got it – wham! I knew I was a gone goose there and then – and about as hopeless 'cause I seen her look at you.'

'Aw nuts! The gal don't even like me. Anyway, we been chinnin' long enough. It's me for the sack, feller, and tomorrow we'll go see if we kin find that "T" jasper!'

But Frank wasn't to be put off so easily; it seemed he wanted to twist the knife in his wound, he went on talking about April long after Lee had made up the stove and rolled himself in his blankets.

133

Chapter 12

A dead stove and a chilly dawn awakened them; they used wood from Clausen's pile and food from Clausen's store to make themselves breakfast before saddling up and following the trail out of the valley. The way out was not nearly so hard to find and follow as the way by which they had come in, but it wasn't an easy trail for some distance, pitching steeply down the mountainside close to the creek and when the creek dropped a couple of hundred feet – sheer, the trail zigzagged precariously down a slope not so far from being as steep. The horses didn't like it and on the worst parts Lee dismounted and led Black Powder down. Frank's horse was smaller and more sure-footed but all the same, when they reached the more nearly level ground, its legs were trembling and both horses had to be breathed–

'Wouldn't like to have to git cows down there,' Frank commented, looking back up the way they had come.

'Me neither,' Lee replied. 'They'd have to be powerful cheap for me to fetch 'em too.'

'What you mean? You reckon this "T" feller used to go and fetch 'em?'

'Could be. We didn't see no pack-horses up in the valley and it's certain no wagon could git up. Clausen had plenty of stores.'

'You figgerin' "T" brung stores when he come for the cows?'

Lee shrugged– 'It's anybody's guess. Don't matter much anyhow.'

They remounted and rode on down the lower slopes of the mountain, the dense tree growth becoming less thick the further they left the towering bulk of the Black Rocks behind; soon they were able to catch glimpses of the prosperous looking range country ahead of them until, with startling suddenness, as they turned a corner in the trail, they found themselves face to face with a small ranch. It was as dilapidated and run-down as the Circle M, but there was a fine looking grey horse tied to the sagging hitch rail in front of the shingle-roof double cabin; the horse carried a silver mounted saddle which looked worth the whole of the ranch buildings together. Lee's eyebrows lifted– 'Visitin'?' he queried.

It was Frank's turn to shrug– 'We better go careful, these back-wood ranches usually do a piece of rustling on the side.'

'Yeah, and they could be tied in with Clausen. Keno!'

Fifty yards short of the cabin Lee pulled Black Powder up– 'Hello, the house!' he called.

135

In the silence he heard a chair scrape over a rough floor and a fat, frowsy looking man appeared in the open doorway that gave upon the drunken porch, he carried what looked like a brand new Winchester and Lee noticed a heavy gold ring on one finger of the hand that gripped the rifle stock– 'Hello, your own selves,' the fat man told them.

'We're kinda lost,' Lee said. 'Kin you tell us where at is a place called Snake Butte?'

'Who'n hell's that, Potter?' another voice asked. The fat man was pushed aside from the door and a small, meagre-faced man appeared; he had eyes as hard and black as agate and a thin slit of a mouth; his long, slender hands were poised over the butts of a pair of long-barrelled Colts which Lee at once coveted–

'A couple of punchers lost, Weaver,' Potter explained.

'Lost? Here? Where are at you headed, Misters?' The voice was sharp and imperious.

'Snake Butte,' Lee told him, 'and if you don't know the way…'

'I know the way but I ain't tellin' every dang saddle tramp that asks. Where you from?'

'I'm from where it ain't healthy to ask questions!' Frank's face went brick red and he made a move towards a gun, a move that Lee checked at once.

136

'We're from someplace else,' Lee said quickly, although his temper was just as near boiling point as Frank's, 'and if you don't like it you kin chaw on it till you bust a tooth!'

'Feller, folks don't talk to me like that!'

'Maybe not until now they ain't. Too bad!'

Weaver drew but Lee had anticipated just that; he had a Colt already out and level before Weaver's guns cleared leather–

'Save it!' he snapped, 'save it for the small town tin horns that maybe think you're fast. Now, where is this Snake Butte place – or maybe it's such a lousy, small dump you got it hidden under your vest!'

There was no element of fear in the hate that blazed from Weaver's eyes– 'You snaked the draw on me,' he gritted.

'Sure I did,' Lee told him easily. 'And you kin put that rifle down, Fatso!'

Potter, whose face had gone a pasty white, obeyed at once– 'And you, Weaver,' Lee went on, 'don't think I couldn't beat you on a straight draw; I just thought you might be partway fast and I didn't wanta kill you. Where's Snake Butte?' His voice crackled on the question so much that even Frank blinked; so far as he had known Lee he'd thought his boss was a reasonably even-going sort of fellow; now he hardly recognised him–

'You're on the Snake Butte trail,' Weaver admitted grudgingly.

137

'Right. Just you and Potter come on outa there and walk a piece down to show us the way. And, Weaver, just shuck your guns, will you?'

Under the steady threat of Lee's Colt muzzle, Weaver slowly drew his guns from their holsters and let them fall to the sagging floor of the porch then, slowly, stiffly, as if they were strangers to the exercise, he and Potter came down the creaking steps their eyes as much upon Lee's gun as upon where they were going, so much so that the fat man missed the last step, slipped, fell, bumping into Weaver who kicked at him viciously. Lee noticed Potter's eyes as he got back on his feet– 'Potter don't like Weaver, not over-much,' he told himself. 'Git movin',' he said out loud. 'I like the look of your backs better'n your faces.'

The ill-assorted couple walked away down the trail, Potter rubbing his side where Weaver's toe had hit him; Lee and Frank followed behind until they were well clear of the cabin then– 'You kin go back now,' Lee told them, 'now that you're far enough off not to pot shoot us with no rifle. Git!'

They got, but not before Lee had seen Weaver's dark eyes blaze with fury.

'Let's ride,' he told Frank, and they urged their horses to a lope. But, to Frank's surprise, they rode for only a couple of miles when, on their reaching a small stream, Lee turned aside up the current, at length pulling his horse away up the bank into a willow thicket.

'How come?' Frank queried.

Lee said– 'Our broncs is tired; Weaver's ain't. My guess is he'll go lickety-split for town, we couldn't stay ahead of him so I figgered we might as well let him go chasin' off while we go back and habla with Potter some.'

'Ahuh. You figger Potter knows somethin'?'

'I'm hopin' so. The place looks purty rundown but he had a good rifle and a new ring.'

'Yeah, could be. Say, Lee, I never knew you could be so tough. Was it an act?'

'No act, Frank. I just nacherly hate Weaver's type, mean-minded li'l sidewinder like I said. I seen a good few like him – cheap skate gunmen makin' a fast dollar by being fast with a gun; crooked enough to screw in th' floor an' always out to rile some chump of a cowpoke into drawin' on 'em. If I hadn't been a fool I'd have shot him then. Quiet now, I kin hear him come!'

They drew further back into cover as Weaver appeared using his quirt on the big grey which, as Lee had anticipated, was going hell for leather. Weaver splashed through the creek, lifted the horse cruelly at the following up slope and inside a couple of minutes the hoofbeats had faded away towards Snake Butte.

Back at the cabin, Potter sat on the porch steps, a scowl on his face and still rubbing his bruised side; he looked up at the sound of hooves, made a move towards his rifle but stopped it when he saw Frank pointing a Winchester in his direction– 'You agin?' he groaned.

'Yeah!' Lee swung down from his saddle, eased the saddle cramp out of his muscles while he built a cigarette– 'We figgered to have a li'l talk with you, Potter.'

Suspicion gleamed in Potter's whisky-dulled eyes, suspicion and a small mount of interest – 'You the law?' he queried.

'We ain't. You got reason to be scared of the law? Frank, take a look around, huh?'

'Sure, boss!' Frank dismounted and sauntered towards the back of the cabin.

'Me,' Potter said, 'I ain't got no reason to be scared of the law. Hell no!' He spoke with such jeering confidence so different from his previous lack of confidence that Lee was instantly suspicious.

'That kind of law around here, huh?'

'What you mean – that kinda law? I'm honest; I work hard for what sort of a livin' I get. Why should I worry about the law?'

'Potter, you are one danged liar! If you ever did a day's work in your life you sure didn't like it well enough to do a second

140

day! This place is so run-down it's close out the other side and yet you got a ring worth fifty bucks and a whisky nose that musta cost you plenty!'

'Pack saddles in the barn,' Frank reported, strolling casually back – 'and five or six pack horses in the corral. Ain't been used recent.'

'Potter!' Lee said harshly, 'How long is it since you packed supplies up to Clausen?'

'Clausen? Who's he? I never heard of him. Hell, Mister, you ain't got no right...'

It wasn't very convincing bluster and it got Potter nowhere; Lee drew a Colt, span it by the trigger guard– 'I ain't the law,' he said, 'I'm a cattleman chasin' stolen stock!' The implied threat, taken in conjunction with a measuring look Frank took at a nearby pine tree, turned Potter's face a yellowish green ''Bout six weeks ago' he muttered.

'Who brung the supplies here for you to take up? Who pays you?'

'I dunno – honest I dunno, Mister! I just work for pay that's all. Someone dumps the supplies here and I take 'em up; feller that brings 'em he thinks they're for me.'

'And Weaver? Where does that li'l rat fit in?'

'Weaver? He kinda runs Snake Butte.'

'He does, huh? What's his business?'

'Business? Wa'al, I dunno – quite; just cattle I guess.'

'Cattle? How come? What you mean, Potter?'

'I never thought about it; he ain't got a ranch if that's what you mean.'

And that was just about all Lee could get out of Potter who didn't appear to have many brains– 'You keep your mouth shut about this, Potter,' he said, as he swung back into the saddle– 'That is if you want to keep a whole skin!'

'Yeah!' Potter agreed sullenly.

'Guess I'll take that rifle of yourn for a li'l way,' Frank said, picking up the weapon. 'I'll drop it a piece down the trail.'

Potter could only glower as he watched his new Winchester being carried away– 'That's that,' Frank said as he threw the rifle into a juniper bush a couple of hundred yards along the trail. 'How you figger that feller?'

'I reckon he told us the truth – as much as he knew,' Lee answered shortly, 'and such as it was it ties in. This rustlin' is clever – each feller concerned in it only knows so much and no more; Jeff just knew the canyon offen the Lansing range, Clausen just did the brandin', Potter just took supplies up to Clausen. There's brains back of this play, Frank, and we ain't found 'em yet.'

'Weaver?'

'Could be though I'd guess not. Weaver's too dang pleased with himself to be real smart; Weaver's the sort of crook that thinks everybody else is just plain dumb. That ain't brains – that's crazy!'

'All the same we better look out for Weaver, Lee. He'll smell one large rat soon's he finds out we ain't hit town afore him – and he could be layin' for us.'

'He could at that, Frank. We'll go careful.'

From then on they went forward with extreme caution; luckily the range opened out not far beyond the creek where they had watched Weaver pass them and they were able to detour so as to avoid the more obvious places for an ambush. Soon the range became more open still, almost desert, with hardly any cover except a few patches of manzanita scrub and some cactus which they were able to avoid with ease. All the same, the circuitous route they had followed meant that the sun had almost set before they caught sight of town.

Snake Butte crouched under a series of tall, red sandstone bluffs, the nearest and highest of which had been eroded by the weather into a shape that a fanciful man, if he had taken sufficient liquor, could just possibly imagine to be similar to the head of a rattle-snake. Crouched was the right way to describe the run-down place; frame-fronted, long unpainted buildings fronted each other down either side of the street as short and crooked as a dog's leg, more than half the buildings being saloons or gambling joints– 'Most makes you like Lansing,' Frank commented as they tied their horses in front

143

of a once gaudily painted saloon whose sign announced it to be– 'Panther's Pizen'!'

'Yeah, and just as dangerous for us as Lansing,' Lee replied as he saw a lounger detach himself from a post further down street and wander away– 'I guess we'll eat first,' he added, jerking a thumb towards a small building which bore the sign– 'Joe's. Good chuck.'

'Right. I never could stand gunplay on an empty stomach,' Frank agreed, 'and mine sure is empty.'

So, at that time of the evening, was Joe's place– 'Kinda early, gents,' Joe told them. He was small, round, with twinkling eyes and a wary smile which did not alter as he watched them select places from which they could face both door and windows. 'You come far?'

'Far enough,' Lee answered. 'What's for eats?'

'Steak, French fried. You like eggs on it? Three – four? Beans an' cawfee?'

'Suits me,' Frank said, 'and bring some catsup.'

'Sure. Like it tasty, huh?'

'Make it double,' Lee said, 'and four eggs!'

The food wasn't long in the cooking and when they were part way through, Joe, who knew that hungry men don't want to talk, came out from his kitchen to sit on the edge of their table. 'Move over, friend,' Frank told him. 'Me, I like to see the door.'

'Sure,' Joe said, and moved to a nearby chair. 'Lookin' for some'un?'

'Could be some'un lookin' for me,' Frank replied equably.

Joe sighed– 'Hope you don't find him here – or he don't find you; it costs to put new windows in; it ain't a month since I had 'em mended.'

'You get a lot of trouble in town?' Lee queried.

Joe shrugged– 'Box D boys come in to paint the town red six weeks ago,' he said. 'One of 'em had gotten himself cleaned in a poker game at the Panther's Pizen and they figgered to take the town apart.'

'And?'

'Town don't take apart that easy; was quite a battle and my windows was some damaged.'

'Box D, they lose any men?' Lee asked.

'None of 'em kilt but two or three hurt purty bad. You lookin' for punchers' jobs?'

'Could be,' Lee admitted cautiously.

'Box D's a good outfit; there's fellers there have worked for Delmer for years.'

'Delmer? He own it?'

'Yeah. He ain't had it long; feller that owned it afore – feller called Dance, he died and willed it to this feller Delmer that was his cousin.'

Frank nodded to Lee as much as to say–

145

'That explains why Potter hadn't heard of Delmer.' Out loud he asked– 'Where at is Delmer now?'

Joe said– 'Why, he's right here in town. Horse threw him and he busted a leg; he's laid up at Doc Rogers' house, seems the bone ain't in no hurry to knit.'

'Guess maybe we'll strike him for a job,' Lee said. 'And thanks, Joe. Hows about a check?'

'Be four bucks.'

Lee handed over the money– 'You know much about a feller called Weaver?' he asked, keeping his voice flat and indifferent.

Joe's face became blank– 'Weaver? Yeh, he's around,' he said. 'That be all, gents?'

Lee nodded, and Joe vanished into his kitchen as Frank lifted an enquiring eyebrow at Lee– 'Funny Delmer should git thrown by a horse same as your brother!'

'Yeah, too dang funny; I'm bustin' my sides laughin'. C'mon let's git outa here.'

'I could use a drink,' Frank said as they reached the dark street; he paused to roll a cigarette and would have lit a match for it if Lee hadn't struck it roughly from his hand– 'You crazy?' he demanded. 'Wanta make it easy for some jasper with a rifle?'

'Sorry, I forgot.'

'Fellers that forgit when they're on a job like this 'un, they wind up in hell 'fore they remember what it was they forgot. I need a

146

drink too. We'll try this Panther's Pizen place. Speakin' personal I figger we're gonna have trouble and me, I prefer to git it over with.'

The Panther wasn't much of a place and showed signs of hard usage from the bullet scarred window behind the bar to the uneven boards of the floor; one poker game was going on in a corner so dark the players must have had a hard job to see the cards; a blowsy woman in a spangled dress that was none too clean, played an out of tune piano on a platform at the back of the joint and there were half a dozen hard-faced characters with their feet on the brass rail of the bar–

'What'll it be, gents?'

'Beer,' Lee told the sullen, bald-headed barman.

'We ain't got no boys' drinks. Rye, bourbon, brandy is all.'

'Make it bourbon – and it had better be!' Lee answered sharply.

The barman eyed him suspiciously then reached under the bar for a bottle, poured the drinks as if he grudged every drop. Lee tasted his then put it down carefully– 'I said bourbon – not rot-gut!'

'That's good bourbon – and fifty cents,' the barman replied, one hand under the bar.

'And I say it's rot-gut,' Lee answered curtly. 'Gimme decent liquor, and take your hand offen that hawg-laig you got under the bar!'

The barman's pale face flushed– 'I'll call the boss,' he muttered.

'Call nothin',' Lee told him, aware that Frank had eased away from him and was watching both the door and the rest of the saloon; Lee couldn't have told why but he was quite certain from the tenseness in the place that nearly every man there was expecting, waiting for something to happen. The poker game had stopped, the woman at the piano had stopped; only a couple of flies chased each other over the glass from which Lee had taken a sip. The barman's eyes fell to the glass as one of the flies settled upon the lip, touched the liquor and fell on to the bar where it lay on its back– 'Powerful rot-gut too,' Lee commented. 'Guess I'd have acted the same if I'd tooken all that drink, huh?' His tongue felt suddenly dry and twice its normal size and for a moment the saloon seemed to spin in front of his eyes, so violently he had to grab at the bar to keep himself from falling– 'Drugged too, huh?' he heard himself say thickly. 'Why you...' Then he felt Frank grip his arm; he shook his head to clear it, and with some success for he had taken only the veriest sip at the drugged drink. The barman's sullen face came slowly back into focus– 'I'm awright now, Frank,' Lee said. 'Awright enough to take this feller apart to see what makes him tick. Who told you to drug the drinks?' he demanded of the barman, and the muzzle of one of his Colts rapped upon the bar to reinforce the question.

The barman, face pasty white again, passed his tongue over his lips– 'I – I dunno. I... That drink's awright! There ain't nothin' wrong with it! It's good likker!'

'Then drink it!' Lee ordered. 'Drink it yourself. Drink it or take a bullet!' His thumb suggestively eased back the hammer of the Colt which was only feet from the barman's belly.

The barman was still trying to make up his mind when the doors crashed open to admit a big, red-faced man who wore a Marshal's Star on his vest, and cradled a double-barrelled shotgun in his arms– 'What's goin' on?' he demanded. 'Hey you – with the gun! Drop it or I'll blow you apart. I'm the law here and the law says all guns should be checked in at the Marshal's office! Didn't you see the notice when you rode inta town?'

With the shotgun's muzzle only a yard from his back Lee hesitated; he could see the Marshal's face in the bar mirror and he didn't like what he saw. It was a whisky face, mottled and seamed with drink into a million tiny lines; the eyes were watery and the Marshal's breath demonstrated that he'd already had more than a few drinks

149

that evening; besides, Frank was off to one side and able to drop the Marshal almost as quickly as that man could pull the heavy trigger of his shotgun; almost but perhaps not quite, Lee relaxed his grip on his Colt so that it rested upon the bar, then half turned so that his body was between the marshal and his other, still holstered, Colt–

'No,' he said, 'I didn't see your notice, Marshal. And as for this – it's just that I don't like the likker they serve in here! I aim to keep the law so I guess I'd better pay a fine for breakin' it. You drinkin'? Maybe if you'll let me buy you one I'll be able to git a decent drink my ownself!'

Thirst competed with evident instructions in the Marshal's eye and in a short time thirst won– 'Yeah, I'll take a drink,' the law officer said, 'but don't think you ain't comin' to jail after, feller. And you too!' He fixed what was supposed to be a beady eye on Frank, but he failed dismally for his glance at once wandered to the drinks being poured by the sullen barman – from a bottle which had been in plain view.

'You kin have this 'un back,' Frank told the barman, and spiralled his drink into the sink; without a word the barman replaced it– 'Luck!' Lee told the Marshal, who scowled and sank his drink with one quick elbow jerk–

'C'mon,' he growled. 'Jail for youse!'

'Just one more, Marshal,' Lee pleaded, and once again thirst triumphed over duty. 'What's this notice you told us about?' Lee asked, as he quietly replaced his Colt in its holster.

'Yeah, tell us about it,' Frank urged as he neatly took the bottle from the barman and refilled the Marshal's glass for the second time–

'What notice? What notice?' the Marshal asked, a little glassy-eyed.

'That's gettin' to be kinda heavy, ain't it?' Lee said in a kindly way and relieved the Marshal of his shotgun which he laid on the bar so that it pointed in the direction of the barman; the Law Officer sank his fourth drink and appeared to brood until–

'You gotta come to jail with me,' the Marshal announced. 'It ain't fittin' for strangers to carry guns in this burg. 'Gin the law.'

'Who made the law? Weaver?' Lee asked.

'Yeh. Weaver said... Hell, I'm the law here! I'm the one who saysh you kin carry guns. I'm...' He paused, looked down at his full glass as though hardly believing it; he lifted it and smelled it as though he'd never smelled whisky before, then drank it down– 'I'm the law,' he repeated, the announcement somewhat spoiled by a belch 'I'm the law'n I aim to keep it.'

'Quite right too,' Lee agreed. 'And Weaver helps you keep it, huh?'

151

'You keep your tongue offen Weaver, Mister,' the barman warned, but he shut up promptly when Lee pushed the Marshal's shotgun round towards him– 'Where at is Weaver now?' Lee asked.

'Right here, dang you! An' h'ist your han's!'

Lee cursed his lack of vigilance as he saw in the bar mirror that Weaver had slipped in through the door and now stood just inside, a Colt in each hand. Lee raised his hands stiffly– 'And you,' Weaver told Frank and, as he did so the Marshal's drink-sodden brain told him the moment had come at which he must back his master's play–

'I got 'em, Weaver!' he bawled. 'I got 'em an' wash goin' to bring 'em to jail!' He lurched away from the bar and got his bulky body between Weaver and his two 'prisoners'. As an oath rose to Weaver's lips both Lee and Frank instantaneously acted as if by arrangement, each shot out one of the two lamps and as the lights went out Lee grabbed the Marshal's shot gun, blazed off both barrels towards the spot where Weaver had been standing, before he threw the weapon at the group of men at the bar who, he had glimpsed, were starting for him. Then he dropped to the floor as the saloon rocked afresh to the detonations of Weaver's Colts. Lee's nose bumped a boot, he grabbed a leg as a whisper of 'Lee?' told him he had hold of Frank.

'Door,' he murmured back as they inched to a side wall; the fight had flared up with the speed of a prairie fire, there must have been men in the room with grudges to be worked off, who had seized the opportunity for the working thereof. There was no more shooting but plenty of other noise to make up for it, yells, oaths, a scream or two from the blowsy woman as the piano went over with a twanging crash, the smash of breaking chairs and the thump of chair legs, crash of glass as some decided to use bottles, and over all there was the shrill, furious voice of Weaver shouting heaven knew what obscenities.

Lee suddenly found he was shaking with laughter– 'Weaver,' he whispered to Frank. 'Let's get him.'

They skirted the walls, the fight swirling beside them, a little light crept in from across street through the swing doors – as they neared those doors a couple of men decided there was more room outside and dived through as Weaver's Colts roared again. Lee caught a glimpse of him in the muzzle flare, near enough to go for him in a flying leap that crushed and smashed the vicious little man to the floor– 'Grab those guns, Frank!' Lee ordered. 'I'll git him!' He slung Weaver over his shoulder and headed for the door on the jump; outside he paused to draw breath as the row inside rose to a fresh peak of violence–

'Where to?' Frank queried, as he picked some floor splinters out of his chin.

'Doc Rogers,' Lee replied. 'We'll see Delmer and maybe git Weaver to talk some.'

'Not that jasper,' Frank said. 'Hey, friend! Where at is Doc Rogers' house?' he asked of a passer-by who was hurrying to gawk at the erupting Panther's Pizen. 'We got a man hurt here.'

'Ain't the only one I'd guess; Doc Rogers' is up street a piece – last house on the other side.'

Snake Butte's crooked street wasn't long, nor was Weaver a heavy man but Lee was breathing hard, and thankful when they reached the picket fence in front of the cabin that looked fairly neat.

The Doctor, who answered Frank's knock, was a small, angry looking man– 'Yeah, bring him in,' he ordered Lee curtly, not waiting to be told anything– 'Who is it this time? Curtis or Nason?'

Lee carried Weaver into the room Rogers indicated, a fair-sized room with a bed along one wall, a bed on which lay a big, heavy-shouldered man from whose face the out-door tan had faded. Along another wall was a couch on which Lee dumped his burden– 'Weaver!' Rogers breathed as the head fell limply back on the raised end of the couch– 'What happened?'

'Bar fight,' Lee replied indifferently. 'He hurt bad, Doc?'

'Friend of yours?' the doctor asked.

'Never met him until today. Friend of yourn?'

Ignoring the question the doctor bent over Weaver but straightened up in less than a minute– 'He's dead,' he said, 'neck broken. We'll need some law.'

'Don't be crazy, Doc!' the big man cut in from the bed. 'Ain't nobody gonna no bitter tears over Weaver. He ain't no loss – good riddance in fact. And as for that drunken bum of a Town Marshal...'

'He was in the fight too,' Frank said quietly. 'He tried to put the arm on us for wearin' guns; said it's agin the law!'

Delmer's eyes were keen– 'It wasn't so this mornin',' he said. 'You fellers driftin' through? Or were you workin' for Weaver?'

The doctor seemed to have made up his mind that Weaver's death was not an occurrence to be deplored; he trotted across to a medicine cabinet, produced a bottle and four glasses which he filled– 'Here,' he said, handing one to Delmer, 'it won't help you get better but one won't do no harm. Luck! Gimme a hand to shift that out – I didn't like him alive and I like him less dead!'

Frank helped him carry what was left of Weaver out of the room; Lee looked hard at Delmer– 'we ain't driftin' through, and we

155

weren't workin' for Weaver. I come here to see you – mostly though I'd hoped Weaver would have talked some. I'm Lee Masters – I own the Circle M over the Black Rock mountains.'

'Glad to know you, Masters; I'm Delmer.'

'Yeah, I guessed that. I want you should look at this!' Lee handed over the note he had found on Clausen.

Delmer read it slowly, then– 'Don't get it,' he said. 'I ain't smelled no rat far as I know. Yeah, wait a minute! I did start gettin' ideas 'bout a week 'fore my horse threw me.'

'How'd that happen?'

'Danged if I know. Pedro was going along as quiet as he always did when all of a sudden – bingo! He went up like a snake had bit him, and me – I'm not expectin' it so I was thrown high, wide and handsome.'

'Lucky you only busted a laig,' Lee told him. 'My brother was killed.'

Delmer leant forward– 'What you hintin' at Masters? Let's have it out, man!'

'There's big rustlin' goin' on on this range, my brother was in it for a spell but he got out and was murdered by some'un puttin' a thorn in his saddle; my guess is you had the same thing happen to you.'

'But why? I ain't been losin' cows – far as I know.'

'I didn't say you was; I'm sayin' the sellin' end of the rustlin' crew is this side of the

156

Black Rocks. I found a way through and I found this Clausen feller. He was part of it.'

'He was?'

'Yeah. He was purty fast and I hadn't no time for fancy shootin'; Weaver was in on it and now he's dead. What idea was you beginnin' to git, Delmer?'

'My foreman – Aitchison – him and Weaver were thick. Aitchison runs a few cows – he's gittin' a herd together, I looked 'em over one day and seen a few I hadn't noticed afore that looked like they'd been drove quite a ways. I asked Aitchison about 'em and he didn't answer up too prompt. He kept his few head up in the li'l box canyon that runs up inta the Snake Butte hills and I don't git up thataway offen – not offen enough I guess.'

'Aitchison,' Lee said slowly. 'Your foreman?'

'Yeah. Good cattleman; he knows cows and he knows this range. He'd been on the ranch 'fore I took over so I kept him on. Why?'

'It's this "T" in the note bothers me,' Lee admitted.

Delmer laughed shortly– 'That ain't difficult,' he said. 'Aitchison has always been known as 'Topeka' – he's from thataway. It ain't nice for a man to find out his foreman's been two-timin' him, Masters, but like I said I'd started to git ideas about Aitchison!'

A silence fell between them as they thought out the implications– 'It's purty clear,' Lee said at length. 'Aitchison brung the cows down from the mountain, hid 'em in his box canyon until Weaver sold 'em. Where's the nearest railroad?'

'It ain't far, twenty – twenty-five miles and an easy drive. Yeah, clear enough. And me sittin' here helpless as a bed bug. What you figgerin' to do, Masters?'

'Settle with Aitchison,' Lee stated quietly, 'and try to find out who's back of all this. I figger I know who done the actual rustlin' but there's some'un further back – some'un with brains.'

'Aitchison should be in here soon. It's Saturday and he usually comes to see me when he's in town.'

'Then we'll have us a li'l chat.'

'Yeah, we'll do that. Meantime, how's about a game of poker? Me and Doc, we've played two card Monte till we're sick of it.'

The doctor appeared to think that a game would do his patient good and rigged up a table at the bedside– 'Plumb crazy about poker, he is,' Rogers explained, 'and I reckon not being able to play has riled him more'n anythin' else – and when a sick man's riled it don't help him none to git better.'

'Sick man – hell!' Delmer protested. 'I just got a busted laig. Five buck openers and one buck raises suit you? Fine! Deal 'em, Doc, and let's have fun!'

'Just three li'l old Queens,' Delmer said triumphantly, laying his cards down one by one with great deliberation– 'Just three li'l Queens, the which same makes your two pair look kinda thin, Masters.'

'Gotta let you win sometimes,' Lee chuckled. 'It ain't good for a sick man to be consistent – even if he does think he kin play poker.'

'I kin play awright but I never seen such cards as I've had. What you done to this pack, Doc?'

The doctor, who had been helping himself liberally to the contents of his medicine cabinet, hiccoughed gently– 'I ain't done nothin' to 'em,' he said. 'They suit me fine – just fine. Ain't that a horse?'

Silence fell as they listened to the sounds of a horse being walked towards the doctor's house, saddle leather creaked as a man swung down, spurs jingled as he stamped the saddle soreness out of his legs– 'Aitchison,' Delmer said quietly. 'You like to leave this to me, Masters? He's my foreman and…'

Aitchison was tall, lean and stringy, with a leathery face and darting, restless eyes. He wore two guns, holster tips thong tied to his legs; he squeezed a smile to his thin lips as he clumped into the room– 'Hi, Boss! Company? How's the laig?'

159

'Aitchison, meet Masters and Lacy – they're from the Lansing range – over the Black Rocks.'

Aitchison flashed one look at them in which suspicion and hostility mingled as he nodded– 'I always meant to see what was on the other side of the hill,' he said, 'but never got around to goin'. Want me for anythin', Boss?'

'Yeah I do. Masters here is come chasin' some cows that were rustled.'

'They fly over the mountains?' Aitchison queried sourly. 'There ain't no trail!'

'There is one – and you know the end of it, Aitchison!'

'Me? You gon crazy lyin' there, Boss? How would I know?'

'Quit lyin', Aitchison. The trail ends in that box canyon of yourn where I seen them cows with a brand I didn't know – them cows that had been drove a long ways! And don't try to pull a gun! I've had one on you ever since you come inta the room!' Delmer moved a hand under his bedclothes and showed the bulge of a Colt; Aitchison's eyes darted round the room as if seeking some way out, the corded muscles of his throat worked as he tried to swallow–

'Who's back of you, Aitchison?' Lee asked quietly. 'We know you ain't but a number in this game. Who gives the orders? Spill a few beans and we could make it easy for you!'

160

'What beans?' Aitchison growled. 'You all crazy? I don't savvy nothin' about no stolen cows. I got my string and that's all!'

'Don't be a fool,' Delmer cautioned. 'It'll be a tall tree and a short drop for you if you don't talk.'

'I ain't got nothin' to talk about – and I got friends in this burg. You ain't nothin' but a Johnny-come-lately here, Delmer. I got friends and I...'

'Weaver?' Lee asked quietly. 'Was he your friend?'

'Was?' Aitchison queried harshly.

'Yeah, was. But he talked before he died, Aitchison, and he told us plenty!'

Aitchison released a tiny sigh and the tension went out of him, 'I dunno much,' he said. 'I was just paid to run some cows with my herd, that's all. Ain't no crime in that, is there?'

'When you know the cows are rustled – yeah!' Delmer told him. 'And you're fired. I don't know what Masters is gonna do about you but the Box D don't want you no more!'

'Who paid you, Aitchison?' Lee queried.

'Weaver.'

Lee shrugged hopelessly. Same story again; just another link to the chain who knew nothing beyond the link to himself–

'Don't help much, huh?' Delmer queried. 'You, Aitchison, you tellin' the truth?'

Threat of the noose had broken clean

through Aitchson's hard crust to the soft inside, there was no doubting the sincerity of his– 'I swear I don't know any more, Boss.'

'I ain't your Boss no more. Didn't Weaver give you no hint of who was back of him?'

'Nary a hint, Mister Delmer; he just paid me for keepin' the cows – buck a week each.'

'How many did you have?' Lee asked.

'Didn't keep a tally, Mister, but up to a couple of months ago they was comin' in right smart. Could have been close to three thousand head.'

Frank whistled softly– 'Quite a steal,' he said. 'No wonder Wilkinson figgered the Flyin' W was gonna be shy a few steers. Who drove them cows, feller?'

Aitchison shrugged– 'Sounds crazy,' he admitted, 'but I dunno. I didn't used to go up to the box canyon every day but sometimes there'd be new cows there and I never seen 'em arrive!'

'And you never took a peek? That's a fool lie, Aitchison,' Delmer threw at him. 'You're a cowman, you'd have seen tracks of them cows crossin' our range!'

'I never did, Mister Delmer! I swear I never did!'

'What you figger to do with him Masters?' Delmer asked wearily. 'Seems he ain't much use.'

Lee said– 'No, he ain't no more than

162

another two-spot; Weaver was maybe a nine – ten-spot. I guess I'll take a look at where he roomed. You know that, Aitchison?'

'Yeah, he had a room back of the Panther's Pizen. He owned the dump.'

Lee grinned at Frank, then chuckled– 'We sure picked the place to turn our wolf loose, huh? Git movin', Aitchison. And don't forgit – one wrong move and it's curtains for you. So long, Delmer! Thanks. And here's hopin' you'll soon be forkin' mean ones again! And thanks for the game, Doc!'

Weaver's room, which they were able to reach without going through the now quieter saloon, was like the man – spare, mean and 'pizen-neat', as Frank put it. The roll-top desk, after Lee had forced it with a knife blade, was also pizen-neat and disappointingly uninformative. There was a tidy pad of tally-sheets from the Lantz Cattle Company, showing that over a period of not many months Weaver had delivered nearly three thousand head of cattle to them at an average price of fifteen cents a pound. Lee whistled as he worked out the figures roughly in his head– 'Put them steers at only two-fifty that's close to a hundred thousand bucks!' he told Frank.

'And that li'l skunk only gimme a buck a week each,' Aitchison growled.

But a further search of the desk revealed nothing to show how Weaver passed on the loot to the astute thieves, and that he must have done or else they wouldn't have gone on supplying him with cows; and a moment later Lee realised that Aitchison had gone. While they had been intent upon searching the desk, Aitchison had eased quietly out of the door.

'I ain't liking this,' Frank said. 'Weaver had friends...'

'Yeah he did,' the sullen faced barman growled from another door which had opened silently behind them and led through to the bar– 'Weaver may be dead but we're bettin' you gents'll be able to tell us enough afore you die so's we kin carry on whatever Weaver's racket was. C'mon in, Topeka, and grab their guns.' But as the barman moved to one side to allow Aitchison to squeeze through he took both his eyes and his shot-gun muzzle off Lee for that fraction of a moment Lee needed to draw and fire; his shot missed, but it went close enough to make Aitchison lurch into the barman and spoil his aim. The shotgun blared – but into the roof, and Frank's first shot settled the barman as Lee's second settled Aitchison. Pausing only to shoot out the lamp, they scuttled out of Weaver's room, raced round the saloon, grabbed their horses and pounded out of town– 'We need grub, and the broncs is hungry,' Lee shouted. 'Kin we make it to Potter's?'

164

'We gotta!' Frank answered, turning in his saddle to look back. 'But easy, Lee. There ain't no rush. Looks like Weaver's pals is gonna be too busy to worry 'bout us. That lamp you shot out set the place on fire!'

Chapter 13

'And where in all hell have you been?' Bella Masters had been at the jug and was partway drunk, partway aggressive, partway seductive, a mixture Lee found a little difficult to sort out; besides, he was tired, hungry and dirty after a hard, unpleasant ride back from Snake Butte. For once he was feeling mean, bitter, all too ready to lash back at such a question from a woman who was, to all intents and purposes, living on his charity–

'I been chasin' up the other end of the rustlin' deal you forced Jeff into,' he snapped back at her.

'Me? Force Jeff inta rustlin'? You're nuts! It was me made him stop it!'

'Then you knew he was doin' it?'

A cautious look came into her eyes as she primped her hair; she poured herself another slug of moonshine before she said– 'I had an idea he was.'

'Then you had an idea who was in it with him?' Lee made it an accusation rather than a question, and in doing so he made a mistake.

''Course I didn't. Jeff never told me nothin'.'

'Don't lie to me,' Lee answered disgustedly – and unwisely.

'Call me a liar, huh? Yeah, that's just like you Masters, pick on a defenceless woman and call her every dang low-down name you kin git your lousy tongues round. It ain't fair. It ain't right! You – you dang great bully!' And she burst into tears, howling like a spoilt, thwarted five-year-old until she shrieked herself into drunken hysterics and brought April running–

'What you been doing to her?' April demanded furiously, as she loosened her sister's stays– 'There ain't no call for you to be cruel to Bella.'

Lee cursed under his breath and took himself off to the bunkhouse where he ate some food in a hurry and a foul temper then rolled into his bunk with a stomach ache and dull anger against Bella for putting him into a false position with April. He snapped at Frank, cursed the cook, bawled out the two other Circle M riders and generally tried to work off his ill humour with such little success that when his stomach ache woke him an hour before dawn he decided that the only cure was a plunge into the creek and clear his head before he went to see Duke Purdy, which had been his intention to do that day.

He pulled on his boots, and not bothering about his gun belts, crept quietly to the bunkhouse door where he paused for a moment to make sure he hadn't wakened the others, when he felt the unmistakable pressure of a Colt muzzle against his spine and heard a low pitched voice tell him– 'H'ist 'em, and keep your trap shut!'

Cursing mentally, Lee obeyed the order, and the instruction given by a prod from the Colt, to walk out of the bunkhouse, across the yard and out towards the corral where the waning moonlight showed two saddled horses. To his amazement one of them was Black Powder who, in Lee's experience, had never before allowed another man so much as to lay a finger on him – let alone a saddle– 'Git aboard,' he was ordered, and heard saddle leather creak as the man behind him mounted also– 'Ride,' the voice went on, 'and don't try no tricks!'

Lee looked round and saw that the man behind him was long, lean, grizzled, and wearing greasy buckskins; he had holstered his Colt and now carried a Winchester one-handed across his saddle; something in the way he held the weapon told Lee he was more at home with it than with a short gun.

They crossed the creek, followed the Lansing trail for some miles then veered leftwards– 'Towards the Flyin' W,' Lee muttered, hardly aware that he spoke aloud until the man behind him said–

'Keep your trap shut!'

168

Again Lee looked back, and this time noticed that a long, lean dog of wolfish aspect trotted at the heels of his captor's horse. In some strange way Lee felt that he was no longer in complete control of Black Powder as he usually was; normally the horse used to some extent to anticipate his wishes as a well-trained, one-man animal will, but now – Lee was sure – the man behind was in control. Black Powder carried him but that was all; the horse was going where the man wanted him to. Lee tried to alter his course by the gentle pressure of one knee but the horse, usually instantly obedient, took no notice. Another thing Lee noticed, Black Powder was scared; he was sweating although he'd come neither fast nor far, and the short hairs of his mane were bristling.

Soon they veered further left and began to thread a way upwards through the foothills of the Black Rocks. It was now full light and looking back Lee caught glimpses of the range; he could see the Circle M, and later on, through a stand of pines, he saw what could only be the Flying W. They rode steadily on for what Lee reckoned was all of three hours before turning up a steep wooded draw which gave upon a narrow box canyon in which there was a pole and sod cabin.

Rough outside, it was rougher still inside; dirty, verminous, and smelly as last year but one's washing. A couple of stools, a big stump for a table, a bunk covered with a pile of stinking bear robes and a rough stone fireplace. Lee sat on one of the stools–

"Bout time I knew what was goin' on,' he said. 'Who're you, and what'n Tophet you mean by bringin' me here?' He now had a good look at his captor for the first time – and didn't like what he saw; for one thing, to judge by the glitter in his eyes the fellow's sanity wasn't any too firmly based. Lee judged him to be one of the surviving trappers who'd grown so used to the wilds he couldn't bear to go back to civilisation, even though the beaver – which had provided reason for his calling – had long since been exterminated. The man had evidently stayed on, earning a precarious living by hunting bears, wolves and coyotes; ranches would always pay something for the skin of any animal that preyed upon their stocks, and in the process the man had lived so long alone that if not mad he was the next thing to it. His dog was almost as unpleasant an object as he was, and just as unkempt; it was a great dangerous brute, more than half wolf, Lee guessed–

'You'll be told,' the Wolfer said, in reply to Lee's question. 'Yuh just stay here; I wouldn't move if I was you– Dan'll pin yuh else!' And Dan, by an eager, rumbling growl, showed he was only too ready to start pinning.

The Wolfer went out but came back in a few moments with a jug of water and a couple of strips of jerky which he dumped on the stump 'table'. 'Ain't no need to starve,' he growled. 'And don't forgit what I said about Dan!' Then he went out again and Lee heard him mount his horse and ride away.

For some while Lee sat on the bunk staring at the dog which had settled down upon its haunches and was watching him steadily; he found that all but the smallest movements fetched a thunderous growl from Dan's throat. That the Wolfer had gone to fetch whoever had given orders for Lee's kidnapping, there was no doubt, nor could he doubt that whoever gave those orders was concerned in the rustling, for Lee could think of no other reason why he should be taken; the Wolfer hadn't even bothered to search him and relieve him of the cash he carried.

Lee chewed some of the tough jerky, drank some water while he considered his position – 'I dunno about you, Dan,' he told the dog, whose bristles rose at the sound of his voice – 'dunno 'bout you but I'm hankerin' to find out about this jasper; maybe I could git away from you – maybe I couldn't.' He fingered one of the bear robes as he spoke, thinking that if he could throw it over the dog's head he could possibly use one of the stools as a

171

club– 'But I ain't gonna try it now,' he went on. 'Could be the Wolfer's gone to fetch the big feller, and me, I'm aimin' to find out just who he is. Wilkinson? Could be – but I reckon not. He's smart but he's mean smart. Brent? Agin – could be but he ain't no cattleman. Naw, there's some'un else back of 'em two, and whoever he is he's wanting to find out about that trail me and Frank found, that's what they wanta know so's they kin start rustlin' again – yeah. An' Frank, what's he gonna figger when he wakes up and finds I'm gone, huh? He gonna be able to trail me here? I wouldn't bet on it, the Wolfer picked lots of hard ground and took care not to leave many tracks; I wouldn't back myself to follow it an' Frank ain't no great shakes on a trail...' Lee's thoughts trailed off into a doze and after a while he swung his feet up on to the bunk and made up some of the sleep he had lost the previous night. His sleep was disturbed, and one of his many turnings brought his hip up against something hard; its sharp pressure was so insistent it woke him up and he found that the twin hammers of an old shotgun were pressing into his flesh. The light was fading but there was still sufficient for him to see that both barrels had been fired and that the exploded cartridge in the right hand barrel had been nicked by an off centre firing pin which had nearly missed the percussion cap–

'Cowin,' he muttered, 'Cowin. This is the gun he was shot with! Yeah, ain't no doubt about it. There ain't no two firin' pins could mark a shell same way.' He fumbled in his pocket and found the cartridge he had picked up on the floor of Cowin's office the first day he had reached Lansing– 'So the Wolfer's gun shot him, huh? And who'n hell told Wolfer to do it – and paid Wolfer for it? 'Cause I'll bet a man like Wolfer wouldn't have done it on his own hook. Looks like the Wolfer does the big feller's dirty work – eh, Dan? Don't s'pose you'd talk even if you could.' Another growl answered him, followed by eager jaws snapping as Lee swung his legs off the bunk, eyes busy searching for some fresh shotgun cartridges.

He tossed what was left of the jerky to Dan, but the big dog ignored it completely– 'Too dang well trained,' Lee muttered as he concealed the shotgun once more. 'That Wolfer he sure knows how to handle animals. Now I kin guess why Black Powder was actin' so strange.'

Twilight had settled into darkness before he heard the approach of two horses; Dan came to his feet in one swift movement, stretched, yawned, but never for a second took his eyes off Lee. Saddle leather creaked, then a voice asked– 'In the cabin?'

The Wolfer said– 'Yeah. Dan's guardin' him.'

'Dan?'

'Yeah, my dawg – Dan.'

The dog gave one short, gruff bark.

'Awright,' the Wolfer said. 'He ain't tried to git away.'

Lee saw a patch of starlit sky as the door opened then a shadow darkened the entrance– 'Git that dang dawg out,' the voice ordered.

The Wolfer gave no audible order but the dog slipped out–

'Masters?' the voice queried. 'I kin see you and I got a gun on you so don't try nothin'!'

Lee could see the man too, though not too clearly as he sidled away from the door, the starlight gleaming faintly on the barrel of the Colt he held– 'It ain't no use tryin' to disguise your voice, Wilkinson,' Lee told him acidly. 'I recognised you by your smell a long time since.'

'And there ain't no call for you to git sassy,' Wilkinson snarled. 'You're in a spot, Masters, and unless you're gonna be sensible you won't git outa it alive.'

'Talkin' mighty brash ain't you, Wilkinson?'

'I'm in the saddle and I'll talk the way I want. We know you found the trail Jeff knew and we want to know it too!'

'Me! I ain't found no trail!'

'Nuts! We know you have. You was four days away from the ranch and you couldn't have been no place else but the trail.'

'Yeah? How come you knew so quick I was back?'

Wilkinson laughed shortly– 'We got friends – and we had the Wolfer waitin' to collect you; it was just luck for him you made it so easy by comin' out to meet him.'

'What friends you got, Wilkinson? Mostly thievin' coyotes don't have no friends – and who is we?'

'I'll do the talkin', Masters, and if you've got any sense you'll lissen close. We had a sweet set-up until Jeff turned sour on us – and you know what happened to him.'

'You murdered him – you bastard!'

'His horse threw him,' Wilkinson replied, his voice ragged as if he was only keeping his temper by an effort. 'He had plenty of time to change his mind – which you ain't! Jeff was warned. Now you been warned. You know the trail he knew, and we kin go on same's before.'

'Which was?'

'You know dang well, Masters. You been pokin' about plenty since you come here. First off we figgered you'd play ball with us, and now you gotta play ball with us or else...'

'Or else what?'

'I'll have the Wolfer set his dawg on you!'

In spite of himself Lee shivered; he knew what sort of a chance he would have,

175

unarmed against those rows of teeth and the whipcord strength of that long, lean body– 'Nice feller, ain't you?' he said, only just keeping his voice steady.

'We ain't funnin', Masters; we been makin' a nice thing outa this and we aim to go on makin' a nice thing.'

Lee decided to play for time– 'You ain't told me who "we" is?'

'And I ain't goin' to. You reckernised me – which is too bad for you 'cause lessen you throw in with us you ain't gonna leave this cabin alive! You got one minute to make up your mind! If you don't throw in with us it'll be just another unfortunate accident – poor Masters got himself mauled by a dawg; of course the Wolfer is plumb sorry – but that ain't gonna bring you back to life, is it?'

'You,' said Lee quietly, 'are one low-down, murderous coyote, Wilkinson! And as for throwin' in with you I'd rather throw in with a snake! And you won't never find that trail!'

'We will! You had your chance, Masters. Sure is gonna be too bad about you!' He backed out of the cabin and Lee, a cold fear clutching his heart, got ready to fight for his life. He slipped the shotgun out stood it ready beside the bunk, picked up a bear robe in both hands as the dog streaked, snarling through the door and leapt straight at his throat. Lee knew that everything depended on the first instant; he held the bear robe up and there was just sufficient light for him to see that dark, deadly streak that flashed at him; he managed to throw the robe accurately over the dog's head, to leap aside and snatch the shotgun and batter furiously at the snarling, snapping fury that thumped the cabin's earth floor. In a perfect frenzy of fear and rage he struck again and again; tangled in the thick robe, the dog struggled valiantly, making enough noise to assure his master he was doing the foul job on which he had been sent, but then a lucky blow from the heavy shotgun struck into the back of its skull and Lee stood shakily back, barely able to stand from the suddenly released tension. There was silence for a moment as Lee struggled to collect his scattered wits, then 'All over?' Wilkinson asked, his voice none too steady.

'Yeah,' the Wolfer growled. 'Dan!'

No answer. Lee gripped the empty shotgun, wishing with all his soul he had been holding a loaded Colt instead.

'Dan!' the Wolfer called again.

'Go in and see,' Wilkinson ordered: 'Maybe...'

'Maybe nothin'. Dan's done the job.' Leaves rustled as the Wolfer's mocassined feet shuffled towards the cabin. Lee moved, stiff-legged, to stand just inside the door; the Wolfer paused in the entrance, Lee could see the ragged fringe of his beard as he leant

177

forward to look inside– 'Dan?' he called, a note of doubt in his voice. 'Dan?' He stepped inside and Lee pushed the shotgun muzzle against his ribs–

'H'ist 'em!' he gritted, and snatching the Colt from the Wolfer's holster he dropped the useless shotgun.

'Dan! He's killed Dan! My dawg!' the Wolfer screeched, and reversing the Colt Lee struck viciously at the back of the Wolfer's neck. As the man dropped, Wilkinson's Colt roared, a bullet plumped through the flimsy cabin wall. Lee shot back instantly before taking proper time to aim but his shot went close enough to make Wilkinson duck and jump for his horse. Lee lined his gun up more carefully and his second shot tumbled Wilkinson down in an untidy heap as he was hauling himself into the saddle; his startled horse spooked, one hoof striking Wilkinson's head.

Suddenly faint, Lee sat down with a thump, leaning back against the cabin wall; almost automatically he broke the Wolfer's Colt, pushed out the exploded cartridges and was reaching for fresh ones when he remembered he wasn't wearing his cartridge belt. That brought him back to himself; he drew several deep breaths, pushed the Colt inside his waist band, heaved himself to his feet and lurched over to look at Wilkinson. Even by the dim starlight the position of the crumpled body gave him little hope that Wilkinson would be able to answer any questions; he straightened Wilkinson out but his hand could find no trace of life when he felt Wilkinson's heart; Lee's bullet had only nicked the man's shoulder, it was the swinging hoof of his startled horse that had killed him.

Lee left him lying there, went back inside the cabin, and after using half a dozen matches he found a battered lamp with a drain of oil in it; the light was dim and smoky but sufficient to enable him to see well enough to disentangle the dog's body from the bear robe and throw him outside. Then he turned his attention to the Wolfer and found that the Colt butt had only stunned him; he dragged him on to the bunk and unceremoniously tossed a bucket of water over him. The Wolfer groaned and opened his eyes, tried to sit up – until the sight of the Colt in Lee's hand made him lie back with another groan–

'What's your name?' Lee demanded.

'So long since I used it – I fergit. "Wolfer" folks call me.'

'Maybe, but I need to know your real name.'

'Why?'

'Gonna take you in and charge you with murder!'

The Wolfer sat up in a hurry– 'Murder? I

ain't never done no murder! You can't pin that on me!'

'No? You shot Ed Cowin. Blew him in half with this shotgun!'

'Not me! You got me wrong, Mister. It ain't right – not after you killed my dawg – best dawg I ever did train.'

'You got your nerve!' Lee told him acidly. 'You set that dawg to kill me and then complain 'cause I killed him. Why dang your mangy hide I got a good mind to pull this trigger – only I hanker to see you swing!'

'Swing? Me? There ain't nobody gonna hang me! I got friends!'

'Yeah? And who may they be?'

A cunning look broke into the Wolfer's crazy eyes– 'You'd like to know, huh?'

'Maybe,' Lee admitted, 'but one of 'em is dead – Wilkinson. You mean him?'

Wolfer spat contemptuously– 'White trash,' he snarled. 'I just done jobs for him when I wanted. I kin handle animals – 'most all animals, and make 'em do what I want – cows and all if I've got me a good dawg like Dan that you kilt.'

'And what other friends you got?'

'I ain't sayin'. You'll find out about 'em effen you tries to pin a murder on me!'

'Murder or kidnappin' don't make no difference, they're both hangin' crimes in this State!'

'It ain't so. I was told different.' For the

180

first time the Wolfer appeared to be worried, and perhaps it was noticing that made Lee relax his vigilance a trifle– 'Then you was told wrong,' he was saying when the Wolfer made his play; he must have had a knife concealed about him somewhere for the first thing Lee knew of it was the gleam of the blade as it leapt at him; he threw himself sideways off his stool, his finger instinctively tightening on the Colt trigger as he toppled and as the Wolfer launched himself off the bunk at Lee.

As he fell, Lee's foot kicked the table and rocked it sufficiently to overset the lamp which smashed on the floor as the Wolfer, intent only on escape, darted through the door. Asprawl on the floor, Lee heard a shrill whistle then the pound of hooves as the Wolfer – already in the saddle – kicked Wilkinson's horse into a gallop.

Lee sat up, cursing his carelessness in not having searched the Wolfer before bringing him round; he then went out of the cabin to look for Black Powder; still strangely excited, the horse hadn't strayed far for the canyon floor was thick with bunch grass, but the animal showed a most unusually odd disinclination to allow his master to mount and span round as he hadn't attempted to do since he had been trained. Not expecting it, Lee was caught with one foot in the stirrup, lost his balance and fell, and was dragged some way into the bush before his foot slipped free. He got to his feet to find one ankle uncomfortably wrenched and a face that felt like a pin cushion from his having been dragged through a thorn bush – and a 'wait-a-while' thorn bush as he discovered when he painfully pulled out the three or four thorns that had stuck in his flesh. Cursing again, he limped back to the canyon, called and whistled for Black Powder. The horse, however, had gone off; Lee heard him neigh once and that was all; by this time too angry to swear he looked round for the Wolfer's horse. That, too, had gone, so making the best of a bad job he went back to the cabin, found some more jerky hanging in the outdoor larder and made an unappetising meal before he rolled into the bunk hoping against hope that the coming of dawn would bring Black Powder back to his allegiance.

Chapter 14

Lee was hot; sweat had caked the dust on his face and neck and had run down in rivulets inside shirt and levis so that his flesh was sore and rubbed; he was almost completely exhausted, his feet felt as though a fire had been lit under each, his wrenched ankle was a focus of pain, he was hungry, but above all else he was thirsty. Black Powder hadn't come back to the Wolfer's cabin, nor had the Wolfer's horse; at dawn Lee had eaten a meal, buried what the coyotes had left of Wilkinson and the dog and had set off, with sullen determination, to walk back to the Circle M. In his unsuitable boots the walk soon became a long penance; he tried to shut his mind to the discomfort, the heat, the sweat and the flies that plagued him, the dust that choked him and to some extent he succeeded; the sun was already going down when he crawled through a mesquite thicket and looked across the valley at his ranch in time to see four horsemen arrive from the direction of Lansing. It was too far for him to be certain but he thought that in the leading rider he recognised Barnes – the Lansing Sheriff– 'So the Wolfer made it to town, huh?' he muttered, 'and he's roused up his friends. If that's Barnes he'll be makin' another play to pin the Cowin murder on me – the yaller-bellied skunk!'

For some while Lee lay watching his ranch, trying to decide what to do; half a mile away the creek ran chuckling in its bed, tantalising his thirst almost to madness, almost but not quite for he knew he'd be crazy even to try to think of crossing the open range until darkness could cover his slow movements. He lay watching, while the sun slowly set, until just before the light when he saw three horsemen ride away from the ranch; he could see them only as dim shapes and, as soon as they were past, he struggled to the creek where he drowned his raging thirst. Feeling almost fresh he again crossed the creek, carefully checked his guns; he had taken a Colt and cartridge belt from Wilkinson's body, and then made a slow, cautious approach to his ranch, circling to approach the ranch-house from the back. He was close under the back wall when the sound of a window opening made him freeze and try to flatten himself against the wall as a gun jumped into his hand; April's voice – barely audible – came to his ear– 'Lee?'

'Yeah,' he breathed.

'Lee, the Sheriff's been here. He's taken Frank away to jail and left a couple of gunmen to wait for you.'

'They took Frank away? Why?'

'He tried to pull a gun and they said he was resisting arrest. They beat him, Lee! Beat him terribly!'

'Swine! And they wanted me?'

'Yes. For murder – they said. I hoped you'd be coming back although I was worried when Black Powder came home alone.'

'He's back, is he?'

'Yes. Lee do you think you can save Frank? They beat him wickedly.'

'I'm gonna try anyhow, April. I need my own guns, food and a horse. Where at are the two jaspers Barnes left behind?'

'I don't know, Lee. They're circling around someplace.'

'April!' Bella's voice, sharp and angry– 'Shut that window! There's a dang cold wind blowing off the mountains!'

'I'll have to go. Bella was friendly with Barnes. I'll get your guns, Lee, and the horse. I – I'll try to bring them down to the willow thicket by the creek – and you'll try to save Frank?'

'Yeah, I'll try,' he told her as she shut the window. He felt, as he sidled away into the darkness, that she had also shut out any hopes he might have had that she was fond of him; there had been no mistaking the tremble in her voice when she told him about Frank, or her tense eagerness that he should save Frank– 'Dang that Frank,' he muttered as he moved, keeping carefully to the shadows, down towards the willow thicket. 'So Bella was friendly with Barnes, huh? That dame knows somethin' I'll bet a man. Could be she was the one that sent word to the Wolfer that I was back. Naw, she couldn't have had time; she could have signalled though, from one of them benches the Wolfer could see the Circle M, and if she held a lamp in a window... Yeah, I'll bet that was how it was done. Bella – Jeff's widow; she drew him into it – I'll bet she did, the bitch!'

Lee reached the willows and crouched down to wait while hunger gnawed at his belly and worry picked at his brain; each step forward he made in trying to get to the bottom of the rustling seemed to get him further into a morass of puzzlement. He was still no nearer finding out the identity of the directing brain he was positive had been working behind the loosely knit but efficient organisation that must have gone quite a long way towards stripping the Lansing range of its cattle; Purdy must have lost hundreds – perhaps thousands – of head, and the owners of the Flying W were due for a nasty shock when they eventually saw genuine tally sheets for their ranch.

Down by the creek the nightly frog chorus tuned up again as they got used to his presence, an owl hooted tentatively then Lee heard the rustle of its wings as it plummeted down upon some small creature, came a tiny squeal followed by silence. Somewhere, not far away, a squirrel chattered angrily, a quail, disturbed by some prowler, rocketed out of its hide with an annoyed tumult of wings; time passed slowly but no April came. Lee began to worry, to calculate what time she would have needed, how difficult it would be for her to get his guns, collect food, to find his saddle, rope Black Powder – and he remembered Frank hadn't had much time to teach her how to use a rope properly– 'Maybe I asked her to do too much,' he told himself. 'Maybe some'un seen her gittin' my things. Maybe Bella...'

He lay quiet, curbing his impatience while the ache went out of his leg muscles and some of the sting out of his blistered feet; two hours passed then he heard it; the sound was a faint but unmistakable; from the house, half a mile away came the cry of a woman in pain. Lee ground his teeth– 'That Bella,' he muttered as he got to his feet, cursing as the pain shot up his legs; for the first score or more steps he lurched and staggered as if he'd been drunk, until his muscles slowly uncramped themselves and started to do their job with far less protest. Even if he had been fit he wouldn't have raced to the ranch-house although twice more he heard a woman cry out, once as he reached the deep shadow of the wagon shed and once as, a Colt in each hand, he crouched on the ranch-house porch–

'It was Lee Masters, wasn't it? Wasn't it, April?' Bella's voice was hard and merciless as a whip. 'Answer up, you little fool!'

Lee winced as he heard the whistle of a quirt, the thud as it landed, the moan of pain it brought– 'Bitch!' he muttered, and felt for the door.

'April, it ain't gonna do you no good, I'm gonna beat it outa you if it kills you! Where's Lee now? Where'd you say you'd take his guns?' Again the quirt, again came the cry.

The door opened at Lee's touch and he edged inside the dark entrance hall, dark save for a strip of light which emerged from under the parlour door; he eased across, holstered one gun to reach for the latch, and lifted it gently, then he kicked the door open as he re-drew his second Colt. April he saw at once; she sat in a hard chair, tied and firmly gagged. Gagged! It couldn't have been her cries he'd heard. Even as he realised he'd been trapped a gun pushed into his side– 'H'ist 'em!' he was ordered, as he heard Bella laugh and throw down the quirt with which she had been beating the chesterfield on which she lay–

'I fooled you, eh?' she jeered. 'Poor dang sap! Fooled by his brother's widow.'

Lee slowly released his guns; after one

split second of madness in which he considered shooting out the light, he looked to his left and recognised the man behind the gun as one of the men from the 'Lulu'.

'That's better,' the man told him, kicking the guns away as another man came across from the hall behind him. 'Neat set-up, huh?'

Lee didn't answer. He had nothing to say, anyhow.

'How'd they git you?' Frank asked; his voice sounded unfamiliar as he hadn't yet got used to the gaps where teeth had been. Both his eyes were bunged up and the shape of his nose had been radically altered– 'One of 'em hit me while the other held me,' he told Lee.

Lee groaned as he eased his boots off his aching feet, stretched himself on the second plank bunk of the Lansing jail– 'They got me easy,' he said bitterly. 'I fell for a trick a kid should ha' seen through.' He told Frank what had happened.

'So we ain't no nearer knowin' who's ramrod of the show?'

'Not a dang bit, Frank.'

'And we're in jail.'

'Yeah. Dunno what they'll throw at you but they got me tagged with Cowin's murder.'

'An' Judge Purdy ain't gonna just up and

189

tell you not to do it again!'

'He sure as hell ain't. I been thinkin', Frank, maybe we ain't played this thing the right way.'

'As how?'

'Wa'al, we been chasin' round openly, catching up with all sorts of loose ends; we found 'em, but they ain't got us no place.'

'Yeah, but how else?'

'We're dang sure whoever's runnin' this has brains...'

'Yeah, but...'

'Wa'al, who around here has brains that we know; who's big enough to swing it?'

'Brent?'

'I reckon not. He'd be just another loose end. Naw, I figger we should have guessed who was the king-pin, and gone for him.'

'Easy to say, but who?'

'Judge Purdy!'

'Him? You crazy, Lee. Why he's...' Frank paused. 'Yeah,' he breathed, 'yeah it could be. But why? I don't see why. He's got this town sewn up and that means plenty dinero!'

'Fellers like him always want more. But there's another thing – he hates Duke's guts and it'd be a fine thing for him to steal his son blind, ruin Duke so's he could git back the ranch he figgers should always have been his!'

'Could be you're right, Lee. But it don't help us now. You forgit we're in jail!'

'I don't aim to stay here, not after I figgered out who's runnin' this racket.'

After a pause Frank said– 'But, Lee, from what I hear the Judge is sittin' pretty, takin' a rake-off from all the games in town – and such. Why would he bother with rustlin'? You kin make a faster buck out of a crooked wheel then you kin outa stealin' cows.'

'Yeah,' Lee said, 'that may be so but the Judge, he's different; he was gonna be a big politician, gonna run for Congress and represent the cattlemen – so he said; then bingo! He ain't got no ranch, and all the other politicians they give him the horse laugh. So what he wants more'n anythin' else is to git the Diamond back. See?'

'Yeah, I guess so. But it ain't proof.'

'I know it ain't, but it's plumb likely and it ties in with the way he treated me. First off he was as nice as pie, figgered I was gonna be easy and go on doin' what Jeff had started doin'. Then he seen I wasn't gonna be easy so he tried the hard way – sendin' Harrison to scare me. I don't scare easy either, so he figgers to wait until he's sure I know what Jeff knew about the trail – and then he slaps me in the can. It's all of a piece, Frank, it's just gotta be.'

'And where does Bella fit in?'

'Could be Jeff got drunk sometime and spilled about this trail he'd found. Bella seen him fix the poker game he won the Circle M in; my guess is Brent had her marry Jeff so's she could keep tabs on him.'

'Sounds all right, Lee, but we are sure as hell still in jail! And there ain't nobody likely I kin think of to git us out.'

'Duke Purdy might try, but he's got his own troubles. We'll just nacherly have to git out our own selves, Frank.'

'Easy talk.'

'Yeah. So shut your trap and let's git some sleep. My feet still feel like I walked over a prairie fire; I ain't in no shape for no jail break right now!' Lee settled himself as comfortably as he could on his plank bunk and went quietly to sleep.

It was day again before he woke up feeling stiff and sore – but much better; Frank's swollen face had lost some of the more unusual of its contours and his stiffness, from his beating, was wearing off.

A surly Deputy brought them both breakfast, and while they ate it they took a good look at the Sheriff's office; the bars which formed the inside of their cell fronted the room in the court-house set aside for the use of the Sheriff of Lansing County; it was a big room, bare except for a desk, one easy chair and a couple of hard ones, and none too clean, with a stale smell of sweat and smoky lamps and gun oil.

The Deputy who had fetched breakfast and who had been on duty all night, soon shambled off some minutes before his relief appeared–

'That's the feller that beat me,' Frank muttered. 'He's my meat. Feller called Ivery.'

Ivery shifted his quid of tobacco, spat at a much missed cuspidor and added to the brown stains round it before slouching over to the cell– 'Teach you to be sassy,' he growled at Frank.

'Brave jasper,' Frank jeered back. 'Big law man. I'm gonna git you for that Ivery!'

'In a pig's ear; all you'll git is a three-foot drop. You had your chance to sing, canary bird!' He slouched to the easy chair, fell back in it and reached around for a whisky bottle that had been hidden behind it, scowling as he held it unbelievingly up to the light– 'That Brand!' he muttered. 'Thievin' swine! I'll have his...'

'Too bad! Too bad!' Frank jeered. 'Big, bold, bad law man had his whisky snitched right outa the Sheriff's office! Tck! Tck! This is gonna git the law a bad name in Lansing when Miz Dobie gits to hear of it!'

To the utter amazement of Lee and Frank, Ivery's face, for a moment or two, went quite pale with anger; he fairly raved at them and ended up by hurling the bottle which smashed on the cell bars and showered glass inside– 'I don't want no sass!' he bawled. 'You lousy coyotes, keep your dang traps shut!'

'Mr Lacy,' Lee said in a quiet, gentle voice, 'you heard the Deputy Sheriff! We ain't to speak, Mister Lacy. We ain't to say one single dang word. Understand?'

'Mister Masters, I git you. You won't hear me say not one solitary word not even to that bow-legged, stinkin', spavined, lop-eared, swivel-eyed, bottle-nosed...'

'Shut up!' Ivery roared, and bouncing out of his chair he rushed at the cell door.

Lee stared at him; it was the first time he had ever seen a man foaming at the mouth – and that was what Ivery was doing; his hands clawed at the bars and he shook them in an absolutely frenzy of rage, rage all so absorbing he didn't notice Frank's hand steal quietly through the bars to his holster and gently remove his gun. He went on screaming at them until Frank hit him smartly between the eyes with his own Colt butt, and he slumped towards the floor– 'He got the cell key?' Lee demanded, clutching at Ivery's vest to prevent him falling away from the bars– 'Grab him, Frank, and I'll search him!'

'No use, Lee,' Frank said, 'there's the dang keys hanging up on the wall over there! I never thought of that one.'

Lee cursed vividly, took the Colt from Frank's hand and tried to look through the bars at the hasp on which hung the padlock controlling the cell door– 'A danged awkward shot,' he muttered, as he eased the gun between the bars, 'but it might…'

'Yeah, might not too,' Frank reminded him. 'Awright if it does bust the hasp, but whether it does or not – it's sure gonna wake the town up!'

Reluctantly, Lee pulled the gun back and whipped it under his vest as Sheriff Barnes came into his office. Barnes' eyes widened as he saw Ivery's body; he scowled– 'Had another of them fits of his, huh? You buzzards musta riled him considerable. Hell! Where's his gun?'

'Right here, Barnes,' Lee said quietly, 'and don't try to reach for yours! This Colt's loaded. Just elevate your hands and ramble over to git the keys!'

Barnes' hands lifted slowly; he hesitated, two fears conflicting in his worried eyes– 'Sharp now!' Lee ordered as the Sheriff still hesitated.

'You daren't shoot,' Barnes stated doubtfully.

'Wanna find out? Git them keys!'

Barnes did nothing– 'You daren't shoot,' he repeated – more firmly.

Lee clicked his teeth impatiently; the last thing he had expected was resistance from the Sheriff whom he'd credited with as much courage as a jack-rabbit. He thumbed back the hammer of the Colt– 'Make with the feet, Barnes!' he ordered. But Barnes only shrugged, backed to his desk and sat down on it–

'You'd be no better off if you did shoot,' he pointed out. 'You still couldn't git the keys!'

He was right and Lee knew it; he could only grind his teeth with anger, realising as he did that it was only a matter of time before someone else came in; and that some-one else did come in – April. She came in with a rush and ran across the room to Lacy–

'Oh, Frank! Your poor face! Are you all right, honey? I – I've been so worried, but we couldn't get in before.'

Barnes saw his opportunity and took it; he left the office on the jump while April was between him and Lee– 'Save the sob-stuff,' Lee's voice crackled. 'April! Git them keys – quick! Those over there!'

The girl did as she was told – and pretty quickly. Barnes was hardly out of the door before she'd darted across the room, snatched the keys from their hook. Luckily the first one she tried was the right one; the padlock opened, the bar shot back and they were out of the cell at least– 'Not that way!' Lee warned as Frank, one arm round April, headed for the street door. 'Some'un'll be watchin' that. We'll try this door!' He headed for a door he had noticed behind the Sheriff's desk; it could have been no more than a cupboard – but it wasn't. Evidently

196

unused for years, it gave upon a short passage at the far end of which a steep ladder led upwards into darkness–

'Where now?' Frank queried, as the closing door shut the light off.

'How'n hell do I know?' Lee answered irritably; the look in April's eyes as she had rushed at Frank told him clearly that all his hopes of winning her were vain. The faint sound of a kiss in the darkness made him only the more irritable as he fumbled his way along towards the ladder– 'You better wait here,' he told them. 'I'll go up and have me a look-see.' As he climbed the ladder he admitted to himself much as he liked both April and Frank, in the present, precarious situation he would rather have had their room than their company– 'Frank'll be too worried about the gal to be spry with his trigger finger,' Lee muttered, and dismissed them from his mind. He guessed that the ladder must at one time, before the Sheriff's office and jail had been added, been fixed to the outside wall of the court-house, for it emerged through a trap door let into the sloping roof of the jail; above, and behind him was the parapet of the court-house roof, and for a few seconds – while he hauled himself over on to the flat roof – he was in full sight of anyone in the street who might have looked up. From the roof he found he had an excellent view, not only of the other side of the street, but also of the court-house side, for the roof went out over the court-house porch and he could see down along the boardwalks. He saw Barnes, rifle in hand, emerge from the 'Lulu' and, followed by three other suitably armed men, cross the street purposefully towards the jail; a crowd had gathered, but oozed quickly away at the Sheriff's approach. Brent was one of the men with the Law Officer, and as they reached the door of the office – which was almost immediately under Lee – he heard Brent say– 'He ain't gonna be pleased about this, Barnes!'

'It ain't my fault Ivery had a fit, is it?' Barnes replied querulously. 'They had a gun on me when I went in – and then that gal…They've gone!' he added.

Lee looked over the parapet; he could have spat into the crown of Brent's hat – 'Course they've gone,' Brent answered savagely. 'Think they was gonna wait for you to come back? George! Skin around to the livery stable and tell Hughes to watch his stock – close!'

'You gonna tell him?' Barnes queried anxiously.

'Me? Hell, no! Why should I? You let 'em git away!'

'They ain't gone far!'

'They ain't gone at all!'

Lee almost jumped at the new voice – it

198

was Bella's and came from almost directly in front of him.

'I seen the Sheriff come out,' she said, she must have been standing under the court-house porch– 'But I never seen anyone else. They must still be inside!'

Lee moved quickly back to the trap and called softly down for the other two; it was a risk that had to be taken, getting them over the exposed parapet, but they made it without the shout from the street Lee dreaded to hear– 'Where now?' Frank asked.

Lee didn't answer; he crossed the roof to the other side and saw, as he looked over, that the roof of the next building – Mrs Dobie's boarding house – was not impossibly far away– 'Kin you make it?' he asked.

Frank looked doubtful– 'I could,' he said. 'But April–'

'I can make it,' the girl said quietly. 'You go first, Frank. Lee can help me this side.'

The other roof was some feet lower and a yard away. Frank swung himself down easily enough but they had much more difficulty with April, her wide skirt made a nuisance of itself and Frank, from the lower side, didn't help matters by averting his eyes with a modesty which in the circumstances, was ill-timed. Lee also swung himself down easily enough, turned away from the edge as Mrs Dobie's sharp voice demanded– 'And what in tarnation are you doing on my roof?' Her head, with its gimlet eyes and wispy hair poking from under her cap, was all that showed above the trap door in her roof–

'We're tryin' to git away, ma'am, and we need help!' Lee told her bluntly.

Mrs Dobie's eyes were upon the generous length of leg April's caught-up skirt left exposed. April flushed deeply and pulled her skirt free– 'Glad to see you ain't a hussy!' Mrs Dobie snapped. 'You better come down – and tread careful. I don't want my roof trampled.'

The ladder down which they followed her led to the back of the hall; she turned and faced them, hands folded and a grim expression on her face– 'You the sister of that Masters woman?' she demanded.

April could only nod.

'She's a hussy!' Mrs Dobie snapped. 'I knew that soon's I set eyes on her. You're different. You kin stay here. You men – you kin stay till it's dark, but no longer!'

Chapter 15

'Had me an idea while I was up on that roof, Frank!'

'Yeah? What about?'

'Bringin' Purdy out inta the open.'

They were kneeling behind the net curtains of Mrs Dobie's parlour, watching the systematic search Barnes was making; Mrs Dobie had swept April away to the back of the house to 'freshen up'.

'Yeah, fine. But how?'

'When I was up on the roof I looked across street into that newspaper office and seen the feller workin' that old roller press he's got.'

'So what?'

'So I kin work one; we used to have one of 'em back in Tracy for runnin' off reward notices and such.'

'How we gonna git over there?'

'Dunno. But we'll think of somethin'. I ain't happy just settin' here and waitin' – and us with only one gun between us.'

Gradually the activity in the street became less; Brent, with a couple of men, went by heading for a down street saloon called the 'Maverick'; Barnes and another pair of gunmen tricked out as Deputy Sheriffs, were away up street beyond the 'Lulu'. Lee heard a distant thud of hooves, the jingle of harness and creak of springs– 'Stage's comin',' he said. 'If she's rollin' fast there'll be a good lot of dust behind her. C'mon Frank! Let's git ready!'

The four horses were pretty tired after their rough thirty-mile stage but the driver believed in doing things with a flourish; he used his whip freely as he neared town, and as he swept past Dobie's he had his team moving smartly, the dust rolling in a high, climbing cloud behind the lumbering Concord. Under cover of that cloud Lee and Frank made it across the street, undetected; they paused for a moment on the boardwalk then pushed through the door into the newspaper office and printing shop of the 'Lansing Examiner.' The Editor, who was also compositor and printer, looked up from behind his fount of type– 'Too late,' he said. 'Can't take no more "copy" – paper's made up purty near!'

'Then you gotta unmake it!' Lee told him curtly.

The Editor's eyes blinked belligerently behind their thick lensed spectacles, the hand that came up from behind the print cabinet held a gun – most cattle country Editors were as handy with a Colt as they were with a stick of type, they had to be or they didn't stay

Editors for long– 'Paper's made up,' he said, as curtly, 'and there ain't no cowpoke gonna tell me different!'

'I want an announcement put in,' Lee told him.

'Yeah? What sort?'

'Just one sayin' that Judge Purdy is one lowdown, thieving coyote that ain't got the guts to come out in the open and uses all sorts of other coyotes to front for him – such as Barnes and Brent to name two.'

The Editor slowly laid his gun aside and pushed his eyeshade back– 'Say that agin!'

Lee repeated what he wanted, with embellishments, while the Editor's eyes – now remarkably keen – studied his face– 'You asking me to c'mit suicide?' he demanded.

'I'm askin' you to print the truth!' Lee replied, 'and I want you should print where this secret trail is; once everybody knows about it it can't never be used for rustling again!'

The Editor scratched his thinning hair– 'What secret trail? What rustlin'?' he asked. 'You're going too fast for me, feller. An' who are you anyway?'

Lee grinned– 'Guess I did sort of fall over myself,' he said. 'I better tell you the story. I'm Lee Masters!'

'I guessed it,' the Editor told him. 'And just so we won't be interrupted...' He crossed to the window and drew the blind down.

Somehow, by reason of that simple action, Lee knew that he was going to get his story printed the way he wanted it– 'My name's Hansom,' the Editor told him, 'and I guess we could use a drink.' He produced a bottle and glasses from his desk, poured the drinks. 'Here's luck,' he said, 'and I guess we'll need it – if I'm crazy enough to print what you said – and maybe I am. I've been getting good and tired of the way Judge Purdy's been running this town and I reckon it's time the 'Examiner' spoke up plain what most honest citizens have been thinkin' for months. Get talking, Masters.'

Lee made it as quick as he could but the story was some time in the telling; Hansom listened in silence, head resting on one hand while he made notes with the other. When Lee had finished Hansom got up, pushed aside the frame he had been making up, took a stick, and whistling softly, began to pick type. He worked steadily for half an hour filling stick after stick with large type until the forme was full; then he locked it, carried it across to the old-fashioned roller printing machine, fed in paper and turned the handle. The first sheets were blurred but as the ink ran more smoothly clearer sheets came off until Lee and Frank were able to read– 'Judge Purdy is a two-timing Buzzard!' the flaring headline stated baldly. 'He ought to be hung!' blared the next line.

204

'Maybe he doesn't pull the trigger but he hires murders done! Who rustled his son's cows?' There was a lot more, a lot of accusations of crimes Lee had never heard of, and the diatribe ended up with a firm challenge that Judge Purdy leave town by sundown that day – or stay and be hung–

'That'll fetch him,' Hansom said, rubbing his hands with satisfaction, 'He'll be over there like a Democrat after votes when he reads that.'

'And I'll meet him,' Lee said quietly.

Hansom shrugged– 'I ain't no fighting man,' he said. 'I fight when I have to but not unless.'

'How we gonna git this to Purdy, though?' Frank Lacy queried.

Hansom pulled the blinds aside– 'Ain't gonna be easy,' he admitted, 'not with all them fellers lookin' for you two. Say, there's Duke Purdy ridin' into town! Maybe he'll help!' He went to the door, opened it and beckoned to Purdy who turned his horse, swung out of the saddle in front of the entrance–

'Howdy, Hansom! Want me?'

'Yeah, Duke. I got a new piece I'd admire you to see.'

Duke tied his horse, eased his saddle stiffened muscles as he got up on the board-walk– 'I heard they got Lee Masters in jail? The skunks!' he said. 'I rode in to see if I

205

could help. Lee! Wa'al I'll be...' He gripped hands with Lee, clapped Frank on the shoulder– 'So you busted outa jail? Guess there's plenty you gotta wise me up on, huh?'

Hansom hadn't quite closed the door and as Duke moved forward, away from it, a skirt rustled, looked in and would have vanished at once had not Lee fairly leapt forward and dragged Bella inside, kicking the door to behind him–

'Lemme go!' she bawled, just before he clamped a hand over her mouth and tried to hold her violent writhings; she fought like a wild-cat, and she was no lightweight but big and powerful; not until Duke lent his aid did they quieten her down. Even then she spat her defiance until they tied her in a chair and gagged the stream of virulent abuse that spouted from her mouth. Lee backed away, sucking the hand she had bitten–

'She in it too?' Duke queried.

For answer, Lee gave him a copy of the 'Examiner'. Duke read slowly, a dark flush creeping up his neck as he read on– 'This true?' he asked.

'Far's we know.'

'Could be. Dad – Dad always hated me, and when Ma left the ranch to me he hit the roof, near to went mad. It could be all this is his doing. Here! You seen this?' He held the sheet in front of Bella's eyes. At first, as she

206

read, her eyes showed only anger but, as she went on fear came into them too, fear followed by a look of cunning. She mumbled something behind the gag and, after a look at Lee, Hansom removed it–

'Ain't such a thing as a drink around here, is there?' she croaked.

Hansom gave her one and she drank it quickly– 'I could be useful to you jaspers,' she said, as Hansom took the empty glass back.

Lee answered her only with a lifted eyebrow.

'Yeah, useful,' she repeated. 'Benstead knew a lot and he...'

'Told you,' Lee prompted.

'You got it purty right in that paper. Judge Purdy wanted the Diamond back, wanted it bad. Brent was in on it with him – and Benstead; they had to take Wilkinson in to make it look better. Been funny if only the Diamond lost cows. Jeff got drunk one night and told Brent about the trail he'd found; I knew Jeff had cheated in the poker game he won the Circle M in so I made him marry me so's I could keep an eye on him.'

'And Benstead?' Lee queried acidly.

Bella shrugged– 'Jeff found out about me and Benstead; he would have thrown me offen the ranch only I knew how he got it; but he quit cold on the rustlin'. They warned him and said he'd git killed if he didn't go on; Jeff said he didn't give a damn – so they killed him.'

'How?'

'You know how. Benstead put some of them thorns in his saddle and Wilkinson sent him that killer horse; if that hadn't done for him the Wolfer would have done. Kin I have me another drink?' She told the story with an utter lack of emotion that was repulsive. Hansom held the glass out to her at the end of his arm, as if he found all contact with her repulsive– 'Wa'al, I told you all you wanta know,' she said, after she'd gulped the drink down. 'Now I want my price!'

'Price? What price?'

'Five hundred bucks. I'll turn State's Evidence for that – and not a cent less.'

'We don't need your evidence, Bella,' Lee told her curtly. 'You'll be in jail with the rest of them!'

'Jail? I ain't gonna go to jail! I – I'll help – I told you all I know. I'll help take them papers round – you gotta git 'em round ain't you? You got to git folks on your side!'

Lee rubbed his unshaven chin; the problem of distributing the papers had occurred to him, but in the excitement of seeing his story converted into print he had pushed it to the back of his mind–

'She's right,' Hansom said. 'Usually I take 'em round my ownself – but not this one!'

'See?' Bella demanded. 'There ain't nobody but me kin take 'em round; I'll do it if you promise I'll not go to jail!'

Lee shrugged, glanced at Frank, and nodded– 'Awright! You win!'

'And my five hundred bucks?'

'The hell with your five hundred bucks!'

'But I need car-fare, and new clothes.'

Frank had cut her free, and as she spoke she stood up, smoothing her dress down over her bosom – 'I gotta look smart to go to my sister's weddin',' she told them, with a meaning glance at Frank.

'Here,' he growled, pushing a pile of papers at her. 'Git movin'.'

'I'll take some,' Duke said. 'I'll do one side of the street.' He picked up a stack of papers, but Lee gripped his arm–

'Easy, Duke,' he said. 'After all – he's your Dad!'

'I ain't none so sure about that,' Duke said surprisingly. 'I was only a baby when Dad went to the war but I was a shaver when he come back and I kin just remember one of the punchers that knew him before say it sure was queer the way the war changed a feller.'

'Wa'al, so it does!'

'Yeah, but not from right-handed to left-handed, huh?'

'Is Judge Purdy left-handed?'

'Yeah. He even cuts his meat with his left

hand.' Duke grabbed his papers, and with a quick– 'So long!' he was out in the street where they heard him bawling– 'Extra! Extra! Read all about it! Extra!'

'Sure got his nerve,' Lee chuckled. 'Git movin', Bella!'

She followed Duke at once, and Lee smiled quietly as he realised that, having gotten over her fear, she was really beginning to enjoy herself; she had sufficient of the actress in her make-up to love the excitement of putting on an act. As her voice joined Duke's, people started coming out of their houses, eager to find out what the excitement was all about– 'Sure would like to be in the 'Lulu' when Brent sees his copy,' Lee thought, and was at once seized with an idea, a preposterous idea but one on which he at once acted– 'They'll be back in the "Lulu",' he told Frank. 'Grab a copy, hold it up in front of your face and ramble back to Ma Dobie's; April'll be worried about you.'

'What you aimin' to do?' Frank asked suspiciously – he was getting to know Lee pretty well by that time.

'Me? I'm gonna stay right here,' Lee said virtuously – but untruthfully.

'Wa'al, awright. But…' Frank strolled out, his face hidden behind a newspaper; Lee watched him across the road then pulled Ivery's Colt from his holster, looked it over carefully.

'Going out?' Hansom asked.

'Yeah. I wanta see how Brent takes it.'

'Figgered so. There's a back way – folks'll mostly be watchin' the street.'

'Thanks, Hansom. That way'll be less risky than walkin' along behind them head-lines o' yourn.' Lee headed for the back door, paused as his hand gripped the knob– 'Thanks for your help!' he said.

'Shucks! I been waitin' to fix Judge Purdy for two years. Me and him, we've hated each other's guts since the first gun at Fort Sumter.'

Lee's eyebrows must have lifted, for Hansom smiled– 'He ain't dared to kill me,' he said. 'I got too much on him, and he knows dang well that if I died sudden it'd go straight to the State Prosecutin' Attorney. Yeah, the Judge don't like me!'

'Seems to me the hell of a lotta folks in this town ain't liked the Judge for a hell of a long time. How come they ain't done nothin' about it?'

Hansom just shrugged, and Lee slipped quickly through the back door, turning left up behind the buildings, ducking below window levels and darting across alleys until he was brought up all standing by a low call of– 'Masters!' His gun jumped into Lee's hand as he turned to face the voice – pure instinct, for reason would have told him the gun was useless, an enemy would

211

have shot first–

'Hell! Taylor!' he said, when he saw who it was. 'You gimme a shock!'

The old gunsmith's eyes, peering keenly through his quarter opened back door, went to the Colt in Lee's hand– 'Lost your guns, huh?' he asked. 'Just when you need 'em most. C'mon in, son.'

Although he grudged the delay, Lee obeyed and went inside to find Taylor pulling out a drawer deep under the shop counter– 'Yeah, went out without 'em,' Lee admitted. 'Dang fool!'

'I knew I still had 'em,' the gunsmith said triumphantly, grunting as he lifted a box from the floor and opened it on the counter– 'Like 'em?'

Lee drew in his breath sharply as he looked down at the finest pair of Colts he had ever seen; automatically his hands took them up to find that they were as beautifully balanced as their appearance promised. 'Like 'em?' Taylor asked, but the question was really quite unnecessary.

'An' how!' Lee breathed.

'Then take 'em! Take 'em and use 'em on that skunk Purdy. Here, I'll find a box of new shells; those there...' he paused and swallowed hard, 'those there have been in the guns four years.'

'Four years?'

'Yeah. Them – them Colts belonged to my

son. I bought 'em for him.'

'An' he never used 'em?'

'A little. He was wild, just young that's all. He got in a poker game, crooked one, and they braced him.'

'Who did?'

'Never could find out. Barnes didn't try too hard.'

'Ahuh. Purdy – you figger?'

Old Taylor shrugged– 'I dunno,' he said. 'I dunno. Folks said he had a share in the saloon where it happened.' He reloaded the Colts, span the cylinders then handed them to Lee. 'Use 'em,' he said, and at once went into his back room and slammed the door.

Lee made half a dozen practice draws with the gold-chased Colts, found they came as sweetly to hand as any guns he'd ever handled, then he eased himself out of the back door, crossed the alley to the 'Lulu' in a couple of jumps, crouched for a few moments under the back window and then risked a quick peek over the sill into a small room that looked as if it was Brent's office. The room was empty, the window a trifle open; almost before he knew what he was doing Lee raised the sash and rolled over the sill. For a moment or so he stood listening, glanced at the untidy desk then shook his head, crossed the carpeted floor to the door; the time had passed when he could hunt for incriminating documents. As his hand dropped to the door knob he felt it move and jumped aside just in time as the door was pushed open almost in his face– 'Yeah, sure, Brent,' he heard Ham – the barman – say. 'Yeah, I'm gettin' it now!'

Lee saw Ham stride to the desk, pick a small box from a pigeon hole and hurry back, leaving the door open; the crack between door and frame gave Lee a slit view of the inside of the 'Lulu' and the ten or so men who had crowded to the front door and windows looking out into the street. Brent was at the bar, opening the box Ham had fetched from his desk– 'Here you are, boys!' he called. 'Deputy's Stars for all of you! Roll up and pin 'em on then it don't matter who you shoot 'cause it's legal!'

'Sure somethin' mighty queer going on out here, Brent,' one of the men said. 'There's the hell and all of a crowd and they're all readin' papers, shoutin' and yellin'. I kin see Duke Purdy givin' 'em out. Yeah, an' Bella too!'

'Bella? What the hell...?' Brent dropped a handful of Stars and strode to look over the swing doors. Ham raised up on tip-toe to see over the heads of the men at the window and Lee slipped quietly out of Brent's office and wedged himself in the back corner of the bar–

'Ham!' he said quietly.

The barman turned, his jaw dropping as

he looked down the barrel of one of Lee's Colts– 'Easy, Ham. Far as you know – I ain't here, see? One peep outa you and...' Lee let the rest of it ride.

Ham nodded, pale-faced, licking lips that had gone suddenly dry; he poured himself a drink and gulped it down– 'Me,' he whispered, 'me, I only work here.'

'You seen the Wolfer?' Lee asked.

Ham nodded– 'He's around. Was in here a couple of minutes ago.' His eyes shuttled back to the door as Brent said–

'Dang bitch! Looks like she's throwed in with young Purdy. She's coming this way!'

There was silence in the saloon, a silence that could be felt; near Lee's head a fly buzzed busily round the lip of a whisky glass, others circled the bottles behind the bar, dust motes danced in the shafts of sunlight, a man cleared his throat rustily– 'Crowd sounds kinda hostile,' he muttered, and Lee agreed with him. It wasn't possible to identify any words but the sound of an angry crowd is unmistakable. Heels clacked on the boardwalk. Brent moved aside from the swing doors– 'I got news for you, Brent! News you ain't gonna like.' Bella's voice, taut and a bit scared perhaps, but cruelly triumphant. 'Here, read this! Read the truth about yourself. And there's some about you too, Sheriff! Here, have a copy boys! They're all free!'

In the silence that followed the rustle of the papers, Lee risked a look over the bar; every single man was reading intently, lips moving with the words. Ham peeked over Brent's shoulder, took one look at his Boss's livid face and ducked down behind the bar, stripped off his once white coat, grabbed a fistful of bills from the till– 'I quit,' he muttered to Lee, and vanished through Brent's office.

Unconscious of the departure of his employee – and the contents of his till – Brent pounded one fist on the bar– 'The dang fool!' he growled. 'The stupid idjet! That trail's worth thousan's and he has to tell the whole dang world!'

'He's honest, Brent,' Bella jeered. 'You wouldn't know what that means, would you?'

'Bitch!' Brent flung back at her. 'So you talked, huh?'

'Only enough to git in the clear – which you never will. So long, Brent! And thanks for the buggy ride!'

Flame and smoke mushroomed at Brent's hip, the saloon rocked to the blast of his Colt; Bella staggered and would have fallen if Barnes hadn't caught her and eased her back into a chair. For a moment or two she tried to struggle then, abruptly, she went limp– 'That was murder, Brent,' Barnes said mildly.

'Yeah, maybe,' Brent snarled, his smoking gun still out. 'And any other yellow rat gits the same. We kin still swing this deal – we ain't done yet. Judge Purdy runs this town – not some half baked dope of a newspaper! Wolfer! You found Masters yet?'

Lee risked another look and saw the Wolfer sidle in through the door– 'I trailed him to your back window,' the Wolfer stated flatly.

'Here? My back window? You crazy?'

'He ain't crazy – you are!' Lee stood up, a Colt in each hand. 'That'll be about all, gents,' he said quietly. 'Just–' And that was as far as he got before he saw Brent's gun swinging towards him and shot instantly. The Wolfer grabbed at his gun but he hadn't got it out before a bullet spun him to the floor with a smashed shoulder; the roar of revolver shots filled the place as three or four of the 'Deputy Sheriffs' shot back; bullets broke bottles on the shelves behind him but the heavy bar counter gave some protection – the wreathing smoke more and Lee made a difficult target by never appearing twice above the bar at the same spot. All the same, they could have got him if they'd tried hard.

The blunt words in the 'Examiner' had struck home in each man's brain, each man must have read– 'This means you!' in the plain statement that– 'Lansing County is going to be cleaned up,' and each man was

217

thinking more of a getaway than anything else. By the time the bolder spirits among the crowd – Duke Purdy and Frank Lacy leading – had burst into the saloon, it was more or less all over. Brent was dead, the Wolfer badly hurt, Barnes had a hip wound over which he was making a huge fuss, and all the rest of the bunch had used the back door.

Lee rose from behind the bar, punching exploded cartridges out of his Colts– 'You missed the fun,' he told them.

'You dang ape! You hogged it all!' Duke bawled. 'Whyn't you lemme in on it? You might have told me you was gonna start a private war!'

'Ain't done yet, Duke,' Lee reminded. 'There's still the Judge.'

Duke's face clouded– 'Yeah,' he said, and was going to say something else when little Danny Phillips made his claim to fame; Danny was nine, a sharp youngster, and it had long been his ambition to be the first to run along the street yelling some important item of news. That evening he was lucky; he happened to be sitting on the boardwalk opposite the courthouse when Judge Purdy emerged. Instantly Danny dropped his copy of the 'Examiner' and raced up street– 'He's comin'!' he yelled. 'The Judge's comin'!' His sharp voice carried well and the crowd outside the 'Lulu' fell quiet, soon they could hear inside; Lee pushed the last fresh cartridge into his second colt, span the cylinder to make sure all the cartridges had seated properly and then pushed the weapon into its holster–

'For me,' he said, and vaulted the bar, to be brought up against Duke's hand pressed against his chest–

'No,' Duke replied, 'for me.'

'Me first – you second,' Lee told him. 'You got a wife!'

'That's a dang fool reason.'

'It ain't. And if he is your Dad?'

'He ain't. I'm sure he ain't.'

'He's comin'!' Danny shrilled, and ran right into the saloon.

Lee pushed Duke aside– 'No more argyfyin',' he said, and strode out into the street.

Judge Purdy was a hundred yards off, the setting sun outlined his bulk and made the details indistinct, but even with the sun in his eyes Lee could see he had a Colt swinging low on his right hip–

'Some'un said he was left-handed,' he muttered, and felt the first stirring of a vague disquiet which became the stronger as Purdy advanced slowly, steadily, remorseless as doom. Seventy, sixty, fifty yards separated them; Lee couldn't see Purdy's face, he could only watch the right hand held, finger stiff, out from his side. Doubt again bothered him. Was Purdy left-handed or was that just another false trail?

'Masters!' The Judge's voice was low but vibrant with anger– 'I been a fool over you. I thought you was a fool – I was wrong. Still, it ain't too late for us…' Then his left had moved with the speed of a cardsharp palming an ace. Lee caught no more than a glimpse of it as it streaked to an under-arm holster; he jumped to one side, his own guns leaping out and up, jarring his wrists as they came level and exploded. Lee felt a bullet tug at his shirt, his hat flew off as his guns crashed a second time. Judge Purdy swayed then fell forward on his knees; he made a tremendous effort to raise his guns again, but failing pitched forward on his face.

Cautiously, Lee approached, kicked the Colt from the Judge's flaccid grip then holstered his own, rolled the dying man on his back– 'Yeah, I underestimated you,' the Judge went on, 'and that pup – Duke.'

'Your son?'

The Judge rolled his head impatiently– 'Son – hell!' he said, his voice so weak Lee could hardly catch the words– 'He's my brother's son – my twin brother. He was killed in the war; I come back instead.'

Blood gushed from his mouth, his body stiffened then went limp.

Lee strapped his bed-roll to the cantle of his saddle, swung up on Black Powder then

220

took a paper from inside his vest and handed it to Frank Lacy– 'There you are, Frank,' he said, 'there's a wedding present for you and April – the Circle M.'

'What'n hell you mean, Lee?'

'My brother didn't come by it honest and it brought him grief – me too. You're gettin' it honest, Frank, and you and April'll make a go of it.'

The publishers hope that this book has given you enjoyable reading. Large Print Books are especially designed to be as easy to see and hold as possible. If you wish a complete list of our books please ask at your local library or write directly to:

Dales Large Print Books
Magna House, Long Preston,
Skipton, North Yorkshire.
BD23 4ND